Childish Ways

Fran Gabaldoni

ISBN: 9798645326043

Cover design by: Rowan Hopkins

For Abby and Rob

Chapter 1

Black Beauty

Me and Thomas Tate are laughing. We can't stop. We're nine years old and about to take a death defying trip on Tom's mum's ancient bike. The bike is massive, and I mean massive. Steel frame, rock solid tyres, metal brakes and the saddle the size of a breadboard. It is black and seven hands high, or something like that. We call her Black Beauty. Three-hundred yards from Tom's house in the quiet and beautiful Cotswold village of Lambe, there is a track. This track leads to the river Evenlode, one of West Oxfordshire's four rivers. It's August 1977 and it's hot, very hot.

The dusty track leads down to the river eventually, but before it does, it passes over a red brick bridge that spans the Oxford to Kenbury railway line, fifty feet below. The drop is massive, impressive and very scary. According to Lambe folk law, for a dare, Dean Taylor once climbed along the very narrow ledge that runs along the outside of this bridge. If he had fallen, he would have died for sure. Dean is now in a young offenders' institution because he got caught syphoning petrol from cars in the village, with his long-term criminal friend, Paul Finn.

The track tiptoes its way over this bridge and starts to descend viciously towards the river. At the top of this hill Tom Tate has one delicately sandalled foot on the pedal of his mum's push iron. His other foot supports his braced leg, which is digging into the dirt to stop the bike cascading down the hill before we are ready.

Close to wetting myself with laughter now, I am sat on the enormous saddle. I will be getting a 'backer' on this short journey: a passenger, nothing more, Tom is driving. He's good at giving 'backers' because he's stronger than me, not much taller, but definitely stronger. The problem is, he is used to giving 'backers' on his own Raleigh Chico, not an adult's bike the size of a penny farthing and less stable.

I was expecting an, "Are you ready?" type call from Tom, but it doesn't come. The first thing I remember is nearly falling off the back of the bike as we shoot off. A fall from this height would probably put me in a wheelchair (although death would probably be a better option when Tom's mum, Edith or Mrs Tate to me, finds out we've nicked her bike to do shit on). I grab onto the back of Tom's new, yellow Ned Kelly T-shirt that his Uncle Tony has just brought him back from Australia.

The laughter has stopped now, this is serious. At the end of the track we have a river to our right, a five bar metal gate to the left and Bridge Cottage bang in the middle; also with a five bar gate, but this gate, thankfully, is made of much softer material, wood.

Absolutely zero planning has gone into this short journey. We haven't thought about it because why should we? Tom's mum's bike has brakes doesn't it? Well, no it doesn't; at least not brakes that can stop a three and a half ton steel object designed in 1845, carrying two nine year olds (even though we are pretty skinny), hurtling down a bumpy track.

The sound that the metal brake cable makes as it snaps is sickening. I reckon it was about as loud as one of those cables snapping on an aircraft carrier, if it breaks when it's trying to catch a plane (I thought of this because me and Tom had been playing Flight Command on his landing at his house yesterday and the rubber bands that act as real life cables kept breaking).

Whilst my petrified mind was distracted by Flight Command, Tom was using all his mental and physical abilities to steer this unstable projectile to safety. A momentary movement to the right suggests the river is the safest option, but this is quickly corrected and we head, at speed, towards the metal gate to the left. Bracing myself for impact, eyes tightly shut, I hold my breath.

Unseen by me, Tom has noticed that the gate is slightly open and although we brush the catch on the gate post as we scream by, we make it through the opening. Yelps of relief are quickly replaced by four wide eyes and two open mouths, as we realise our ordeal is not over.

Calamitously, the other side of the gate offers a further navigational challenge; made possible by years of tractor tyres making ten inch parallel canyons either side of a foot wide plateau, leading twenty yards down the track. At the end of the track a lush green meadow awaits a soft landing. The canyons, however, offer certain death. We have to steer for the plateau, or we're dead, for sure.

Tom, unbelievably, manages to guide us onto the plateau but it's like riding on a tight rope, two up! The margin for error is six inches either side of our bike wheel, which might seem a lot, but not when you're travelling at warp speed! A huge wobble (probably created by me) has surely put a premature end to our stupid, short lives but Tom corrects again and with screams of laughter we finally come to rest, after a small skid and a minor fall, into the safe arms of the meadow.

Dusting ourselves off, we check the bike for damage. Nothing more than a bust cable (that we will deny all knowledge of if Mrs Tate asks, or we'll just blame Tom's brother, Jim). We'll need to smuggle the bike back into the garage, but we should get it back before Mr Tate returns from Thorpley private school, where he teaches RE.

As we push the bike back up the track, the day still hot, we look at the obstacles we have just avoided. The biggest being Bridge Cottage. Tom turned to look at it.

He says, "You know Dean Taylor and Paul Finn robbed that house once and nicked all their money and killed their cats?"

I nod.

Chapter 2

This is hell. Absolute hell. This is my Somme. My concentration camp. My coffin.

It's three fifteen in the morning and I'm lying in a bed on the fifth floor of Bristol Children's Hospital, oncology ward. The constant low moaning from the six other beds is punctuated by an occasional scream. The regular beeps from machines drown out the sobbing coming from the bed in the corner opposite ours.

I'm lying on my back, on my 'pull out of the wall' bed, staring up at the solid wooden casing that the bed folds back into when it's not in use. In the dull, neon, orange light of the ward, it looks like I'm staring up at my coffin. Beside me, in bed one, is my daughter, Emma: one and a half years old, my baby, golden haired, beautiful. Pale, so very pale. White. Seven hours ago she was diagnosed with leukaemia. Acute lymphoblastic leukaemia to be precise, whatever that means.

Emma had been a bit poorly for a while: couldn't shake a cold, grumpy, not settling, not eating very much. Normal stuff, kiddy stuff, you know? It was when she coughed up a tiny bit of blood, which lightly stained a tissue, that everything changed.

"Better get an appointment with the doctor," we'd agreed.

"Nothing major, just a bad cold and a viral infection," said the doctor from Lynford surgery. "Time and cuddles, that would do it."

A few days later I go for a walk up the drive with her. She toddles along getting to the end of the gravelled drive holding my hand, but there's no way she's getting back under her own steam. Out of breath now, face one colour, pale; less than that, no colour.

It's Saturday, so the doctors' are shut. We decide to take her to the small community hospital right in the middle of The Wye Forest, where we moved to nine months earlier from North London. It's a great little hospital, the sort that Tory Governments try to shut down all the time, but local resistance actually means something around here and they've never closed it. I went there two months ago, when I attempted to cut my finger off with a chainsaw when cutting up a tree that had fallen across our drive in a storm. My cut was gruesome and almost made me puke but the veteran nurse bandaged it up and, in a well-meaning way, basically told me to, "Stop being a big baby." We live in the middle of a working forest, lumberjacks are in here most days with severed arms.

I'd gently strapped Emma into her baby seat in the back of the black Ford Focus. Alex, Emma's three year old brother, reluctantly clambered onto his booster seat. Louise, my wife for five years, belted him in and got in the passenger seat. Emma moaned.

Dr. North saw us almost immediately, the hospital wasn't

very busy. A quick examination and a passing comment about the small bruises on Emma's body, arms, legs, everywhere really. I hadn't noticed those. I felt a bit embarrassed; the doctor probably thinks we batter her! But the doctor was lovely, she said, "I'm sure it is nothing to worry about, but I would like you to go to Gloucester Hospital for a quick check-up, just routine." She went into another room and the four of us waited for a couple of minutes until she returned. "When you get to the hospital, go to the children's department and give this letter to the doctor on the ward. I will let them know you're coming." She handed me a white envelope which I took without much thought. We thanked her and as we were leaving she replied, "Good luck."

Emma moaned in Louise's arms.

Gloucester Hospital children's department is pretty ropey really. A prefab building that probably should have been replaced years ago. The four of us trudged in and I handed the letter to the nurse at reception. She was very pleasant and found us a quiet spot on the ward, with a cot for Emma. Alex was being great and went off to the playroom with Louise.

A doctor appeared and Louise returned with Alex. He introduced himself as Dr. Meak, which easy to remember because he had an enormous, pointed nose that reminded me of a beak, Dr. Beak. He was in his early thirties and said he just wanted to take a tiny bit of blood from Emma to do a little test. The nurse behind him stepped forward and gently, gently prepared Emma for her first 'bleed.'

It was March and the early spring sun was shining directly into our little corner of the ward. The soporific effect of the warmth, my comfy armchair and the nurses quietly going about their business, on the less than half full ward, made me sleepy.

Louise woke me with a hand on my shoulder, and I found Dr. Beak (sorry, Meak) and a taller, older doctor in a suit and tie standing next to him. I stood up. I saw Alex in the corner of the ward playing with a train.

"Hi," the taller doctor said with a kind smile. The nurse who had taken Emma's blood, I noticed, was quietly drawing the large curtain around our little area. "My name is Dr. Moore," he continued, "And I'm one of the consultant paediatricians here at Gloucester. I'm afraid we have some very difficult news for you about Emma."

So that is why I'm here, staring up at my coffin on the oncology ward, in Bristol Children's Hospital, in March 2003. My world has fallen apart. Completely. My little girl has cancer. She groans, in pain. That's the thing you see, not only is she going to die, for sure, but she is in pain. I'm going to watch my eighteen month old daughter dic, in pain and there is nothing I can do about it, but feel sorry for myself.

Chapter 3

The Passage

Linking my house to Tom's house is The Passage. This Passage is a simple footpath that is neatly made out of grey stone, edged with red brick. It's about three feet wide and it's very important: it takes me to and from my best mate's house and it delivers him to mine. This path isn't very long; it would take you three minutes to walk it, one to run it. When I step out of my front porch, I step directly onto this path and it leads me straight to Moss Barn, the Tate's home. Dotted along The Passage, on either side, are probably a total of fifteen Cotswold houses (apart from the Thatcher's house) of various sizes. I love this Passage.

Let's start with the house opposite ours, Church Cottage, which belongs to the Fairbrothers. It is a cottage, but it's massive and Harry and Pam and their two boys (who are much younger than me and my brother) live there. Harry is a lawyer, I think, but more importantly, he's a fire eater. He learnt it in a place called Abu Dhabi or somewhere, and he showed everyone his skill at the Lambe carnival last summer. I always wondered how they did it, but I saw him drink white spirit and spit it out at the flame. It was still ace though. We like Harry.

Next up we have the Thatchers. Now they are a couple of old mental cases. They moan at my parents when my mum and dad park outside our front door to unload our shopping. The miserable buggers say we block them in.

Two great things to say about the Thatchers and they both involve my mum. One snowy year, me and Tom chucked loads of snow balls at their front door. We had planned this assault like a military operation; although, as it turned out it was about as well planned as Arnhem (note: I'd just watched A Bridge Too Far with my dad). We got caught and Mrs Thatcher grassed us up and I got a bollocking off my mum (even though mum said we just shouldn't have got caught, which basically meant she was glad we did it). And, secondly, when Mrs Thatcher came and knocked on our door for some moan or other, my mum told her to, "Go away, you OLD WITCH!" I was in the kitchen at the time pretending not to hear. I gave mum a little smile when she came back in; she winked back at me. I have never before (or since) heard my mum talk to anyone like that.

The Thatcher's ugly, modern monstrosity of a house is out of place on my Passage and it should be blown up. Anyway, they didn't stay long in Lambe and later a gay man with an illness moved in. He was nice, but he died.

The next house on the right is the Richmond's house. Mr Richmond is an Anglo-Indian furniture restorer and his wife, Marjorie, is a hairdresser. Well, she isn't a hairdresser but she cuts mine and my brother's hair. Well, I say cuts our hair, but I'm not sure she is qualified or authorised in any way to go near children with a pair of scissors. They live in the only thatched roofed house in the village. We get our hair butchered in the Richmond's kitchen every couple of months, so I never get to see the rest of the house, but I always think it smells weird.

One spring day my brother came home with a bad haircut

and tears of laugher rolling down his cheeks. At tea he told me and my mum (dad wasn't home from work) what he'd seen. Sat on a kitchen stool while Mrs Richmond went about her dirty business on his mousey hair, my brother could clearly see the garden and the game of Swingball that was about to commence between Mr Richmond and their only son, Phillip. Mr Richmond was probably in his fifties when he had Phillip, so he was well old to be playing with his seven year old son. Mr Richmond was wearing his usual beige suit, tie and red jumper. He wore this for work and play it would seem, along with a pair of brown slip-on shoes, the ones with a gold bar on. The game seemed to be going on quite well, until Phillip connected with a super forehand and from his low position sent the ball high over to his dad's side, at about head height. Not sure if he should smash the ball back or let it go around again, Mr Richmond got caught in two minds and ducked slightly. This allowed the string (that connects the ball to the post) to slice off his toupee (that everyone in the village knew he wore) and send it scurrying to the ground. Quick as a flash he scooped up the beast, placed it back on his head, shouted, "Two-all," to his son and carried on playing. Exceptional.

The Perkins are next up on the left. Their house is set back slightly off The Passage. Brian Perkins, the son, is in mine and Tom's class at primary school. He's got yellow skin because of jaundice or something and has been pretty ill. I quite like Brian but he isn't a close friend. The thing is, he does have air rifles! He has the high powered jobbies with telescopic sights, not the cheap ones with bent barrels. I love shooting air rifles even though I'm not very good at it (I can't wink my right eye for some reason and because I'm left handed I can't line up the sights very well). My mum and dad would never let us have an air rifle and I will never tell them that me, Brian and Tom shoot black birds out of enormous cedar trees in the Foxwell's garden that backs onto the Perkins' house. The Foxwell's house is a huge mansion house at the far end of The Passage. Its gardens are massive and stretch all the way along the back of the houses lining The Passage. The Foxwell's land basically runs all the way from my house to Tom's house.

Joan and Ted Perkins are Brian's mum and dad. Ted works in a car factory in Oxford and Joan works at Brown's Farm in the village, picking potatoes and stuff like that. Ted and Joan between them smoke about seven-hundred fags a day, and on the rare occasion that I go into their house, I have to negotiate a thick smog of Embassy fumes before I can find a chair to sit on. The Perkins are good people though. I have been told by Tom (who is a closer friend of Brian's than me), that Mr Perkins has, over the past fifteen years, inch by inch, moved his garden fence back into the vast estate of the Foxwell's property. As I've said, the Perkins' small (but ever increasing) garden backs onto the Foxwell's land and this cheeky acquirement by Ted Perkins has, to date, gone unnoticed. Oh yes, one more thing about the Perkins' house. When pheasants find their way into their garden shed, Mr Perkins and Brian shoot them in the head at point blank range, with Brian's air rifle. I'm not judging them or anything, but I'm not sure I'd want to see that.

The Perkins' house marks the halfway point up The Passage. Opposite them on the right-hand side is a big house with a walled garden. I don't know the name of this house and I don't know who lives there, but bang in the middle of this garden is a single apple tree. I don't know what type of apples they are but they are the best scrumping apples in the village. I always find scrumping both terrifying and exhilarating. I regularly scrump apples from this garden, often with Tom or my brother but sometimes solo, just to keep my hand in. I've never been caught at this particular location, although I know many who have.

Ten yards further up on the left you have the Samuels' house. They are Jewish and they have one son called Joseph. Joseph is a kind of funny looking ginger kid, he's a couple of years younger than me and Tom at school but he is super, super, super clever. Cleverer than most grown-ups clever. His mum is a vegan or something, she always looks a bit ill I think. The Samuels' house used to be an antique shop and one of only two shops in the village. There is only one shop in the village now, and that is the next stop on our Passage tour.

Bullocks' shop is run by Mrs Bullocks and it is basically a sweet shop. There might be a Mr Bullocks and Bullocks children, but I have never seen them. Bullocks' shop is in a row of small cottages on the left-hand side of The Passage, which takes you almost all the way to Tom's house. Bullocks' is the perfect little village shop. Sweet jars line the dusty bay window. To the left of that window is a small door, which leads you into a flagstoned, dark corridor. Ten paces down the corridor, you enter another small door on your right. Once through this door, you have a large wooden counter in front of you; where pocket money is exchanged for liquorice pipes, refresher chews, bonbons and, whilst still in primary school remember, ten No6 and a box of Velvet matches. I'm not joking.

Mrs Bullocks would appear through a doorway that has, hanging down from it, those blinds made out of lots of multicoloured strips of plastic. She is probably seventy years old and always wears a blue pinny, like the dinner ladies wear at school. She pads slowly across the flagstones and makes her way around the back of the counter, still with the plastic strips from the blind, draped around her head and shoulders. The strips gently drop away and rustle back into place across the doorway, as she reaches the centre of the counter, directly opposite her customer. You were always fortunate to be in this shop, but if you were really lucky and had silver coins rather than brown ones in your hand, you could do something extra special and ask Mrs Bullocks, "Can I have a look on The Tray, please?"

"Yes, you can dear," was normally the reply (she was friendly but not over friendly) and she would shuffle down the shop and return with The Tray. Now, The Tray is, I guess, just an ordinary tray that people like the Thatchers might eat their tea off whilst watching the telly; it is nothing special. But it is loaded, absolutely loaded with sweets from the Gods of Confectionary! (Mrs Bullocks, the 'Goddess of Confectionary,' I'm not sure about that). Anyway, because the choice is enormous and the whole point of The Tray is to offer you a wide range of goodies, it can often take minutes before you have chosen what you want. Once you had decided though, it was interesting that Mrs Bullocks would always return The Tray to its rightful place, before she came back and took your money (almost as if the Sweet Gods needed to check what had been taken and nod their approval to our shopkeeper).

However, Mrs Bullocks' operating system of *return The Tray before taking your money,* is deeply flawed. Many children in the village (who are considerably braver than me) take advantage of Mrs Bullocks', rather pedestrian, amble down the shop to return The Tray. When her back is turned, the little Artful Dodgers quietly and quickly lean over the counter and grab a handful of sweet offerings on the other side. They pop them in their pockets and still have time to offer up an angelic smile, as Mrs Bullocks turns and heads back up the shop towards the thief. She then takes their money, wanders off again to the till, back turned, and a second dose of shoplifting takes place.

I love this shop, of course, but it was the scene of one of my most heart stopping moments and a roasting off mum. It must have been a couple of years ago because I was in Miss Beard's infant class at school, I guess I was six or seven. My mum had picked me up from school at three o'clock and, for some reason, I had told my mum, as we walked home, that I had been given a gold star by Miss Beard. Oh yeah, I've just remembered why I had said this. My mum had set up a deal whereby every time me or my brother got a gold star, she would buy us something from Bullocks' shop.

"Excellent, well done," mum had said and gave me some coppers to get something little (not from The Tray). As I came back down the dark, cool corridor with my two gobstoppers, I could see my mum silhouetted in the bright doorway. I couldn't see her face until I got outside but as I blinked in the sunlight, I could see that she had her, "I'm very disappointed with you, young man," face on. Next to her was my cow of a teacher, Miss Beard. The truth was soon out: no gold stars had been given out today, least of all to me. Gobstoppers removed from hand, marched down The Passage, bedroom, reading book, silent tea, repeat shameful event to dad when he got home from work.

We are nearly at the end of my wonderful Passage, where my best friend awaits me. Just a couple of places/people of interest in the final third of this wander up my traffic-free walkway. My mum's best friend in the village lives next door to Bullocks' shop: Delia. There are two things to say about Delia:-

1. She is a Quaker and,

2. She is the nicest person ever to have walked the earth.

1 & 2 might be related.

Next to Delia are the McDougals. Mr and Mrs McDougal are both Oxford University Lecturers or something clever like that and they are pleasant, but slightly odd. The main reason I say this is because they haven't got a telly. They have two daughters, Stephanie and Samantha but they haven't got a telly. Both the girls go to a private girls' school in Headington, so we don't know them very well, and they haven't got a telly. I wondered what it must be like for the girls not to have a telly, but it made me feel sad, so I stopped thinking about it. I never feel sad.

Me and Tom gave Mr McDougal a nickname. It's not a cruel nickname or anything, it's just a word that he says (the only word I've ever heard him say, actually). He says it in a very posh, staccato (I know this word because I have piano lessons), high pitched way. The word and his nickname is simply 'Hello.' 'Hello' has a very strange habit; he picks up dog-ends around the village. He's quite tall and thin, has a pointy face, long nose and has glasses. He wears a jacket and tie all the time, even on the weekend. My dad says he's an academic, whatever that is. My dad likes academics, I think, but I have never seen him speak to Mr McDougal apart from exchanges of "Hellos." Mr McDougal looks like a man in my Roald Dahl reading book.

So, that's The Passage, give or take a few houses of non-interest. I suppose there is one other important place right at the end of The Passage, on the left opposite Tom's house; Lambe Primary School. Anyway, I'll pass that by for now because it's the school holidays. It's 1977, it's still August, it's still hot and I'm sleeping over at Tom's house tonight.

Chapter 4

When Dr. Moore had told us that Emma has leukaemia in Gloucester Hospital, he explained that we would need to go to Bristol Children's Hospital where Emma would receive treatment immediately. An ambulance was already waiting to take her. I hadn't cried yet, I simply could not take it in. Louise, strangely practical in these situations, phoned her parents to look after Alex. Eventually, I plucked up enough courage to phone my mum and dad to tell them the sickening, unbelievable news. I cried now. Five years later I would again be mustering up the courage to make another difficult phone call to my beloved parents. They are still living in Green Cottage in Lambe, in Oxfordshire, where they brought me up, and said they would come straight to Bristol Hospital and meet us there.

Louise's parents, Geoff and Jean arrived within an hour. Devastated, they bravely did the practical things that I was incapable of doing at that moment and they took charge of my little boy, Alex. Vulnerable little Alex. What affect was this going to have on him?

With Alex in the care of his grandparents, the plan now was that Louise would go with Emma in the ambulance and I would follow on behind. Arrangements were made with Bristol and I watched Emma be gently loaded into the ambulance and Louise, grim faced, climbed in. Two women in their late twenties made up the crew who were to escort my precious cargo down the M5 towards Bristol. I followed in the car with thoughts of disbelief. How many dads have to do this? Jesus Christ, am I really following that ambulance, with my daughter in, who I've just been told has cancer. Is this really happening? Is it?

I followed the ambulance the thirty miles or so down the motorway into Bristol, where we peeled off under the brightly coloured lollipop statue outside Bristol Hospital, and into the underground car park where the ambulances unload their sick consignments. The ambulance crew helped Emma and Louise into the hospital and directed them where to go.

Someone should always be employed at hospitals to park the cars of dads, who have just followed an ambulance with their dying daughter in. But this is real life and I've got to find a fucking car parking space and, great, I haven't got any money. I ask the ambulance girls where I can park; they can see I'm in some distress and give me directions. I explain that I haven't got any money and, unbelievably, without a second thought, they each give me a handful of change. I cry again.

Trying to find a parking space in Bristol is a headache. Trying to find a parking space in Bristol, around a busy hospital, is stressful. Trying to find a parking space in Bristol, around a busy hospital, when you should be with your daughter and wife on a cancer ward, is breakdown inducing!

I finally shove the car somewhere barely legal around the back of the hospital, misread the instructions on the meter (it's free after 6pm) and feed the hard earned ambulance crew's money needlessly into the machine. I run down the hill and after a few wrong turns find the entrance to the hospital. It's the opposite of Gloucester Royal Hospital this one: bright, new, shiny. Wallace, from Wallace and Gromit, talks to me as I finally get into a lift. "Going up," he tells me all northernly. "Level 5, Gromit, oncology unit (where yu kids cumm to die!)." I hardly laughed at all.

I disembarked the comedy lift at level 5 and followed the overhead signs to paediatric oncology. I know I'm in the right area because a kid (I can't tell whether it's a boy or a girl) shuffles passed me down the corridor. They are wearing a dressing gown, pyjamas and slippers. Oh yes, and they have no hair and a thick yellow tube inserted into one nostril. They are pushing a machine attached to a stand that has wheels. The child trundles passed, ignoring my weak smile of acknowledgement. Welcome to hell.

I quickly find the ward and push the door to get in. It's locked. I look around for a buzzer, find one, push it and wait for a response. After a short delay, I explain that my daughter's just been brought in, "She has leukaemia." The words choke me up completely. The door unlock buzzer sounds and I have to take a huge breath before pushing the door and entering our new, nightmare world.

Emma is already in a bed with something in the back of her left hand, with a bandage around it. Louise is sitting on the bed and we hug. "What's happening?" I ask.

"We're waiting to see the doctor," she says surprisingly calm. I give Emma a kiss, she looks terrible, crying and moaning. I take a look around our new environment. There

24

are six other beds with six kids in them, all younger than ten years old, I would say. I've been working in and around hospitals for the last ten years, albeit as human resources manager, so I know what wards look like. But this is different. The beds are occupied by very little sick looking kids and one of them is mine. It is mind blowing. Parents are around most of the beds but not all of them.

A young male nurse pulls the curtain around us and begins to explain what's going to happen next. Basically they are going to take some more blood and do some much more sophisticated tests, to determine the type of leukaemia Emma has. We will know the result in the morning and a consultant oncologist will come and talk with us first thing. Just then my mum and dad arrive and it's tears all around again.

Chapter 5

The Tates

I'm in my second home, Moss Barn. I spend at least as much time here amongst the Tates as I do in my own home. Tom comes to my house loads as well, but I reckon I spend a bit more time here. There are six Tates. Edith is Tom's mum; a bit older than my mum and a little bit scarier too. Saying that, if my mum and dad got eaten by alligators when doing their weekly shop in Witney, I would go and live with the Tates, no problem. My brother would have to sort himself out somewhere else, I guess.

Edith is a nurse, like a matron, I think. A bit like the one in the Carry On films in the dark blue uniform. She's not fat though like that woman, but she's not as funny either, you can't be everything. Royston, Tom's dad, is much older than Mrs Tate, he's almost a grandad sort of age. He is tall and fit though and he reminds me of the man in the film Paper Tiger: David Niven. Mr Tate is a lot older because Tom is number four in the Tate children line-up. First up is Philippa.

She is flame haired and much older than me and I hardly ever see her, even though she does live at Moss Barn. We were watching Wimbledon last summer in the Tate's telly room. Martina Navratilova was playing and just as she won the first set convincingly, six-one against Betty Stove, Philippa pointed out to her parents that, "Navratilova is one of those homosexuals, you know?" Knowing nods followed from the other five Tates present. I just stayed still and stared at the telly.

Second up is James Tate or Jim. He's much older than me as well and he has got a CB radio. The Tates have an enormous aerial around the back of their house so that Jim can do his CB radioing. "10/4 for a copy big buddy." It's like The Dukes of Hazzard in Jim's room.

You remember that bridge I mentioned on the track down to the river, that massive one that Dean Taylor walked across? Well that bridge was the scene of Jim Tate's worst childhood incident. Walking back after mucking about down at the river last year, me and Tom came to the bridge and there was a full scale catapult war taking place. Either side of the embankment, just below the arch of the bridge, two teams of thirteen and fourteen year old lads in Jim's school year, were having a live rounds battle. Stones were whizzing passed us as we looked down on the assault from the bridge. The teams were made up of about five teenagers each and the distance between them was about fifty feet; about the same as the drop below them to the railway line.

Jim was on the team on the left-hand embankment. At the top of the brick embankments there are, kind of, trenches that offer our marksmen some degree of protection; but you had to put your head over the top to fire your weapon with any sort of accuracy. This 'game' was, of course, absolute madness and was only going to end badly for someone, however, for me and Tom watching these older lads being super naughty, was five star entertainment.

The battle raged for about five minutes; me and Tom had moved behind Jim's team's trench, just about out of harm's way. Suddenly, there was a shout from the bridge above Jim's team and incredibly, a boy from the other team had run across the bridge and was aiming straight down at Jim from about five yards away. Unbelievably, he fired... There was no noise, but the small stone missile hit Jim clean in the mouth. Eyes and mouth wide open in utter amazement, Jim slowly turned his head towards me and his brother, Tom. There was a big black hole where his right front tooth used to be. Time stood still. There was absolute silence for a few seconds, followed by screams and swearing.

"Oh shit, sorry Jim!" The catapult culprit said.

"You fucking idiot!" Was the reply from a member of Jim's team. Jim was sobbing and angry and the battle was obviously over. Nine boys in massive bell-bottomed jeans and tight T-shirts stood about, awkwardly, kicking the dirt on the bridge as Jim, me and Tom walked passed them and up to Moss Barn to face Edith. I didn't know the bad-sport-boy who aimed at Jim from point blank range and I never saw him again. I could only presume he was from another village, Stonesford probably.

Samantha is Tate number three. She is about two years older than Tom and just starting secondary school. I cannot remember ever having a conversation with her, ever. However, I do know that I have a little crush on her. There, I've said it and it won't get mentioned again.

Nice family as they are however, I am here only to dick about with Tom, and tonight I am staying over.

Chapter 6

We are allowed to stay on the ward as long as we like. All night if we wish, which is why I'm lying next to Emma looking up at my coffin. Louise has gone to Clic house which is about a ten minute walk from the hospital. It is a large house where despairing parents of cancer riddled kids can stay in relative comfort, whilst their children undergo twenty-four hour care and treatment. Clic is a charity and apparently stands for Cancer and Leukaemia in Children, and it is a great relief that we can stay so close to Emma, rather than travel the hour journey back home to the Forest each night. Mum and dad went back to our house to sleep, to make arrangements to look after Alex, who, last night, stayed at Louise's parents in Newport. Tonight, our first night, the first night of the rest of our lives, our ground zero, I have decided to stay with Emma in the ward. Emma moans.

It's morning, six thirty or something God awful and I haven't slept at all, not for one minute. The night nurses are on constant duty: comforting parents, settling restless children, cleaning up vomit, changing things on the beeping machines. Christ, the beeping machines. Every few minutes high pitched alarms seem to go off and don't stop until a bleary eyed, though endlessly patient nurse in a light blue uniform, fiddles about with the machine. Emma is attached to a drip to keep her hydrated as much as possible. A cannula, I think it is called, is under those bandages on her left hand and this is attached to a tube that in turn leads to a machine that slowly, slowly feeds the saline liquid directly into her veins. This is the same type of machine that I saw the sickly looking kid pushing up the corridor, when I first arrived in paediatric oncology, twelve hours earlier. The alarm on Emma's machine has gone off three times in the night. It didn't wake me up because I wasn't asleep, it just scared the crap out of me every time it went off because I had no idea how serious it was. It turns out that Emma only has to move slightly and the tube gets blocked and the alarm sounds. It isn't serious but it takes ages for the busy nurses to get around to fixing it.

Morning brings home the horrendous reality of Emma's (and our) situation. Whilst the ward is modern, it is so noisy. There is a cacophony of children crying, nurses and doctors busying themselves and inconsiderate parents with their tellies blaring. "Inconsiderate parents," did I really say that? Give them a break. The parents can do what they want for Christ's sake, their kids are dying. Our kids are dying. My kid is dying.

I get up and give Emma a kiss, she is listless and stinky. I need to change her nappy again. I've never minded changing the nappies of my kids, but I have normally done it in the privacy of a bathroom or a bedroom. I'm on an open ward and her stench cannot be masked by the curtain that I pull around the bed. The muck in her nappy is vile and it takes ages to clear up. Emma is very grisly. I find a bin, dump the filth and go off to the bathroom to clean up, have a wash and sort myself out. I haven't eaten anything since B.C. (before cancer) was diagnosed back in Gloucester, but I'm still not hungry.

Louise arrives about eight o'clock and is tearful. Emma's tummy is distended and it looks very bloated, tight and uncomfortable. I notice a tall, slim, serious looking doctor in his fifties, talking to the ward doctor and nurses by the low level nurses' station, that I can see through the window behind Emma's bed. The doctor has a brown cardboard file in his hand with a few bits of paper in it and as he closes it, I can clearly see written on the outside: EMMA, Bed 1, Leukaemia, Paediatric Oncology, Bristol Children's Hospital.

The tall doctor, a nurse in a dark blue uniform and two other men (who I presume are doctors) approach our bed and my anxiety level rises. He looked at Emma for a brief moment (who was thankfully asleep at last) and turned to Louise and me.

"Morning, is it mum and dad?" he says. We nod. "My name is Professor Elmwood and I am a paediatric oncology consultant." A Professor, I know it's serious, but a Professor!!

"The nurse is going to keep an eye on Emma," he continued, "But I need to talk to you both, can you come with me and we'll find somewhere to have a chat?" The Professor stood back and then ushered us passed the nurses' station and into a small meeting room. We say nothing. One of the other doctors entered the room as well and the four of us sit down around a small round table. The door is closed quietly by the nurse who stays outside. I am numb.

Chapter 7

A night at Tom's

Me and Tom met almost immediately after we arrived in Lambe in the summer of 1971. We were both three; Tom was one month older than me and we went to the same (there is only one in the village) pre-school playgroup, in the chapel down by the playing fields. I can't remember much about our very early days as a duo. However, on our first meeting, I do remember that he wore a yellow and white jumper, had thick, dark ginger hair and had a very big head.

Now, six years later, in 1977, we are both nine years old and we cannot be separated. I am sleeping at Tom's tonight and we do this just about every week in the school holidays. The Tate's home, Moss Barn, is an old house (though not as old as mine), is pebble dashed and is painted white (though it does look a bit green in some places). It has some steps that lead up to the blue front door that is covered by a big porch, with square pillars either side.

Downstairs, Tom's homely house, has one window on the left (the room where we eat our lunch and tea) and a window on the right (the room where we watch telly). There is a small kitchen at the back and a larder room that leads out into a big garden, three times the size of mine. It has a small orchard and a big dusty, high ceilinged garage, almost like a barn. Upstairs there are three or four bedrooms, I think. Tom has his own room, so I have no idea where the rest of the Tate children sleep; I've never asked and I am not interested. There is a small bathroom upstairs and a small cloakroom downstairs. A wizard lives in this cloakroom, in the airing cupboard, to be precise.

I arrive at about four thirty with just a toothbrush. I wouldn't have brought that but my mum gave it to me as I left the house. I've got some pyjama's here because I stay over all the time. Mrs Tate washes them and they smell slightly different to my other clothes that my mum washes. A nice smell though.

We have tea in the Tate's front room at about five thirty. On the wall is a bluey/greeny/white painting of horses pretending to be waves, crashing against a beach. I've seen this painting in someone else's house as well but I can't remember whose. Me, Tom, Samantha, Jim (Tom's sister and brother) and Mrs Tate sit and eat. Mr Tate is still working at his school and I have no idea where Philippa is. I had my sixth birthday party in this room, and I cried when everyone sang, "Happy birthday to you, squashed tomatoes with poo" etc. I knew that everyone was only joking and I didn't have any enemies around that table (or anywhere else actually), but I cried anyway. That's the only time I've been upset in the Tate's house.

Tonight we have pork chops, mashed potatoes, peas and gravy. Mrs Tate is quite a good cook, better than my mum but nowhere near as good as my dad. Me and Tom eat our tea quickly because we've got stuff to do before we have to go to bed at eight thirty.

Sleepovers at Tom's follow a similar pattern after tea. We take our ice lollies (Mrs Tate makes her own out of orange squash) and go and sit outside on the front steps, overlooking the school playing field. Tonight, as we greedily suck our lollies that are melting super quickly in the still warm evening, we have a serious discussion. The topic: Which crown is best?

a) The crown we saw at the Tower of London on a school trip last term, or,

b) The crown in the film The Man Who Would Be King that Daniel Dravot wears, before he is chucked off that bridge.

We both agree that the Tower of London crown is very nice: lots of diamonds, fur and purple velvet, but probably better on a queen. So we agree that Daniel Dravot esq's crown is the best because it is really simple, very heavy and it is made of solid gold. "Oh yes, by Jove." As Billy Fish's character would say in the film.

After we have finished our lollies we go inside and put our lolly sticks in the kitchen bin and wash our hands. We go out through the back of the kitchen, through the larder room and swing out into the garden. We head off down to the back of the garden to the garage and each pull open the large wooden doors, which are twice as high as us. The evening sunshine rushes in and fills the garage with a beautiful, late summer sun. Streaks of dusty light shine through small holes in the walls and ceiling. We go to the back of the garage where the Battle Wagon lives. The Battle Wagon is a Tate family exclusive. No one has anything similar in Lambe, or, as far as I know, in the rest of the world. It's a one off. It is best described as a trailer, I guess. It is about five feet long and has four wheels on which sits a tub, about two feet off the ground and it easily accommodates two nine year olds. At the front, attached to the axle, is a handle about three feet long. Apart from the tyres, it is all made out of metal. We walk passed Black Beauty, which is propped up against the wall on the right. The bike has been turned the other way around to where we left it, those few days earlier, but nothing has been said, so we both shrug and pull out the blue Battle Wagon.

Tom grabs the handle of the Battle Wagon. It turns easily and is pulled out of the garage onto the long drive, which runs along the side of the garden. It isn't particularly heavy and can be pulled along by a small boy at speed, whilst another small boy sits in the tub, hanging on to the sides. And that is what we do for the next half an hour. Taking it in turns to run up and down the Tate's drive, weaving around stuff, going flat out, and basically trying to turn the thing over, which is pretty rare. Although racing is the main activity with the Battle Wagon tonight, it has also, over the years, been used as a picnic table, as a camp and as a canoe (in the garden).

Sweaty and dusty, we pull the Battle Wagon back into the garage. There is plenty of space in the garage because Mr Tate's Datsun Sunny sits, ugly, at the top of the drive near the road. He only sometimes puts this cream coloured monster in the garage (although I think it should be permanently locked up). I went on a holiday to Cornwall in that car with the Tates last summer. Tom's parents in the front, with Me, Tom, Jim and Samantha crammed in the back (I had no idea where Philippa was). It took about four days to get there, at least it felt like that because Mr Tate is a terrible, terrible driver. He isn't scary or dangerous, in fact he is quite the opposite. He drives very, very slowly and comes on and off the accelerator pedal, on and off, on and off, so by the time you reach Stonesford, the next village out of Lambe, everyone, apart from Mr Tate, is ready to puke. We had a great holiday when we finally got there, though.

If you have never played The Lava Game, you've missed out. The Lava Game is a me and Tom invented game and we have played it at Tom's house ever since I can remember. All you need for this game are some stairs. We are in our pyjamas now and we have got about half an hour before bed time. The rest of the Tates are watching telly in their front room and outside that room, in the hall, is where our game begins.

A volcanic eruption takes place in the downstairs cloakroom (the one where the wizard lives) and as it does so, red hot lava begins to flow, very slowly under the door and makes its way to the bottom of the stairs. Me and Tom are the heroes of this game and in it we are called Mac and Bill (not sure why, we just are). As the lava approaches our position near the bottom of the stairs, our job is to save each other from the clutches of the rising lava, as it makes its way up the stairs. It can take ten minutes before we reach the top of the Tate's very steep, carpeted stairs. Sometimes we make it, sometimes one of us doesn't make it and sometimes neither of us make it. It's just the way we play it out.

After two goes at getting burnt alive, we head down the stairs for a third go but this is interrupted when Mrs Tate says we have to go to bed. However, we have a special treat tonight because it is Friday; me and Tom are sleeping in Mr and Mrs Tate's bed and they have a telly in their room that we are allowed to watch until 10pm! (I have no idea where Mr and Mrs Tate will sleep tonight).

Teeth brushed, we settle in: me on the right and Tom on the left of the double bed, to watch the New Avengers. It's a brilliant episode; Purdey and Gambit are in a real life, deadly game, against a man hunting them down, who has gun with a laser on it. They finally turn the tables and get the man with the gun with some karate kicks, but Purdey collapses and Gambit sees that she has been shot with the red laser and there is a deadly mark on her neck. The only way she can survive is with an antidote, or something, which Steed finds and gives to her. Purdey, with her head on Gambit's lap, comes back to life (to my great relief). I really, really like Purdey. There, I've said it and I won't mention it again. Lights out.

Chapter 8

Professor Elmwood opened the cardboard folder with Emma's name on it and placed it on the table. He was a handsome man, with dark skin and a compassionate face. It was still early morning but his tie was loose and his shirt top button undone. He looked like he had already done at least a day's work.

"I'm afraid Emma is very poorly," he said. Louise and I held hands on top of the round table. "We have done some more tests on the blood, that we took from her last night, and I have personally checked the sample and I can confirm that she has acute lymphoblastic leukaemia or A.L.L. Emma is going to need immediate treatment at this hospital. Her condition is very serious but A.L.L. treatment has improved recently and seven out of ten children with her condition do survive."

He continued, "It's a very rare illness, and Emma's chances of getting it were about one in every fifty-thousand children, however, there was nothing that you could have done to prevent it. We're still unclear exactly why children get leukaemia and whilst it is likely to be genetic, it may also be environmental." He paused in the acknowledgement that we were struggling to take all this in. Already I was thinking about the three out of ten kids who don't survive.

"Leukaemia is a cancer of the blood, whereby the bone

marrow, for some reason, creates too many white blood cells. These leukaemic white cells basically take over the red blood cells in the body. Red blood cells carry oxygen and give us the pinkish colour to our skin. This is why Emma has been so tired, because of a lack of oxygen, and her complexation has been so pale. These have been normal symptoms of leukaemia.

"What about the bruises?" I interrupt.

"The bruises are also normal," The Professor explained. "The white leukaemic cells take over the cells or platelets that help our blood to clot. The bruises are basically bleeding, you see." I nod, though not fully understanding the biology.

"Emma is going to need chemotherapy which is very intensive and, I'm afraid, does have a number of side effects. The treatment can cause her to be very ill and unfortunately she will, I'm sorry to say, lose her hair. As I've said, we will need to start her course of chemotherapy today, because obviously the quicker we start the treatment the better and therefore, I need you to sign these forms." He removed two green forms from the folder and placed them on the table with a pen. I signed them immediately.

Putting the pen down, I ask, "How long is the course of chemotherapy?" The pause that followed my question was probably only a few seconds, but it felt like hours.

"It's three years," came the bleak reply. I let go of Louise's hand and slump into my chair, already feeling defeated.

Chapter 9

Halloween: Part One

The summer holidays are over; they simply went on forever, which was fantastic. So, we are back at primary school now and that's fine because I quite like primary school, and anyway we have a couple of major events in my village to look forward to in the next few weeks. Halloween and bonfire night. Two exceptionally fun nights which are outdone only by the build-up to them.

Halloween planning has already started; me and Tom like to get ahead of the game. First of all we have to go to Oxford on the smelly Worth's coach. Our destination: the covered market off Magdalen Street. The covered market is home to the best joke shop in the world (although I've only ever been to this joke shop, I can't imagine that there is a better one). The joke shop is called The Joke Shop and it lives in the far corner of the market, between the butcher's shop (with its pheasants and rabbits hanging all over it) and the Dr. Martens' boot shop.

The Joke Shop is on two levels and the items that we need (to make Halloween the pant wetting, funniest night of the year), are on the first floor. An iron, spiral staircase winds its way up from ground level and delivers you onto the old, creaking, wooden boards of the first floor. Nestling, mischievously, in the far left-hand corner are the three products of joy that we have come the twelve miles from Lambe for: Devil Bangers, Fart Spray, Stink Bombs. That's it: no stupid costumes, no scary masks, no silly teeth.

The Fart Spray and the Stink Bombs are next to each other (naturally) on the middle shelf and the Devil Bangers are just above them. We have both been saving up and have exactly enough money to buy:-

- 1 can of Fart Spray
- 8 Stink Bombs (2 boxes of 4)
- 3 boxes of Devil Bangers (that's one box of Devil Bangers each and one for an experiment that we have been planning for sometime and will carry out when we get back home).

We head off down the stairs, wasting no time with the comedy eyes or the pointy hats. A shopkeeper appears and we pay him, leave the shop and head for the market exit. I take in the smell as we pass the butcher's shop - some people don't like the smell of butchers' shops but as far as I'm concerned they are wrong, I really like it.

It's quite bright as we come out of the covered market and we head off down Corn Street, where we have to catch the one forty-five coach back to Lambe. It's only one fifteen though, and we've already had lunch at Wimpy, so we decide to do something quite naughty, that we were going to do next month, on a special trip to Oxford. However, as we've got time, we may as well be naughty now.

We turn off Corn Street and head towards the ABC cinema where we (and everyone else from school/the world) will be going to watch a film called Star Wars in December. It looks great, I've seen the clips on Tiswas on Saturday mornings. Before you get to the cinema, however, you go down a cobbled side street and next to a big church is Argos.

Argos is a favourite shop of ours because it has....pens. Loads of them. Blue, mini biros resting in the little troughs on top of the slopey desks, where the catalogues are sitting, chained down. The pens, however, are 'free'. 'Free' in that they are not nailed down and 'free' in that we are about to take as many as we can without getting caught.

***

In the seven minutes that it takes from entering Argos' automatic doors, to the time that we leave, my blue Parka coat pockets and Tom's green Parka coat pockets are brimming with plastic and ink.

The heist was a bit easier than we thought it was going to be, but it was still terrifying. I am not a shoplifter, in fact I've never actually stolen anything from a shop. The naughtiest shop behaviour I've done (apart from this) is change the price label on a Spitfire Airfix model, in Woolworths, in Witney. Tom, on the other hand, has taken the odd thing here and there, but he is in no way a habitual thief, like some kids.

There aren't many shop assistants in Argos to catch us because they are all behind the tills. However, there are plenty of busybody customers ready to give you an evil stare (at best) or a, "Stop, Thief!" shout (at worst). However, our light fingers didn't raise any alarms.

We are out of the shop now and break into a spontaneous sprint and head back passed the church, up the cobbled street and dive into an alleyway on the left-hand side. No one has followed us. We've got ten minutes before the coach comes, so we decide to take a look at our booty. We sit on the floor with our Parka hoods up and count.

When we have finished, we both puff out our cheeks and blow: in total, we have an extraordinary fifty-seven pens. I've actually got six more than Tom but it wasn't a competition, it was a joint mission and we have succeeded with flying colours. With no thought or idea of what we will do with them, we grab handfuls of the stumpy pens and stuff them back into our pockets: we casually walk out of the alleyway, head for Corn Street and catch the coach back to Lambe.

Forty minutes later we are getting off the smokey coach at the bus shelter on Woodstock Street, which is about a five minute equal distance walk to either mine or Tom's house. As we head off down the road with a bag each of Halloween goodies and pockets stuffed with pens, Tom turns and looks at the bus shelter, the only bus shelter in village, and says, "You know Mark Hawkins' dad?"

"Yeah, Terry Hawkins," I reply.

"Yeah, well he slept all week in that bus shelter when Mrs Hawkins wouldn't let him back in the house." I nod, knowingly, and we headed off to Tom's house to prepare for the Devil Banger experiment.

Chapter 10

Professor Elmwood got up, but before he left the meeting room he explained that his colleague, Dr. Dickens (who was the other doctor sat around the table), would be about on the ward all day if we had any further questions. Dr. Dickens smiled at us both: he was in his mid thirties, fit looking and bald. "Please, just call me Jim," he said. "I'll try and answer any questions you have throughout the day." Professor Elmwood excused himself, saying he would see Emma on his ward round tomorrow morning and he left and quietly shut the door.

"I'm sorry, it's a lot to take in," Dr. Jim continued. "But we will do all we can for Emma. For the time being, she will stay on the ward but we will try and get her into a side room if one becomes available. I'll discuss with you the treatment we will need to give Emma this afternoon, but in the meantime, you can stay with Emma on the ward for as long as you like, and one of you can stay during the night." I was already battle weary from my first night in the trenches and knew that Louise would have to do the next shift.

Dr. Jim picked up the forms I had signed, opened the door to the small room and Louise and I filed out. Dr. Jim said he would see us later and went to the nursing station and discussed the forms with one of the nurses. Louise and I stood in the corridor and cried.

After we pulled ourselves together, we went to Emma's bed, where a nurse, I hadn't seen before, was taking blood. I noticed that the cannula and bandage were now on her other hand.

"How is she?" I asked thoughtlessly.

"Ok," came the reply. "But her cannula had to be changed, it had already stopped working."

"Is that normal?" I ask, slightly agitated.

"Yes," the nurse said. "They don't last very long in the little ones, I'm afraid, their veins are pretty tiny". Emma's discomfort at having her hand bandaged with a needle sticking into it was obvious. She was restless and whiny, I was tired and hollow.

I had a little sleep in the corridor around lunchtime while Louise watched Emma. I woke up with a start, not quite sure where I was and then the grim reality hit me like a bolt of lightning. I rubbed my eyes and headed back to bed one to find Louise and Emma fast asleep. I finally felt a bit hungry, so I dragged myself off to find the canteen, which was two floors below. As I got into the lift and listened to Wallace doing his thing, I realised that this was the first time I had left the ward since coming here almost twenty-four hours earlier. It was Sunday.

***

Dr. Jim Dickens sat us down in the same small room that we had been in a few hours earlier and he began to explain the treatment that Emma was to receive.

"Emma will have a few different chemotherapy drugs," he explained. "These include Dexamethasone, Methotrexate, one called Vincristine, as well as a high dose of steroids. She will have these medicines in a very regimented way, everyday and the immediate aim of these drugs are to wipe out the leukaemic cells that are causing the damage. The longer term aim of these drugs is to ensure that the bone marrow does not continue to produce these cancer cells, and this is obviously important to ensure that the leukaemia doesn't come back."

"Is he saying, 'Cancer,' 'Leukaemia,' 'Cancer,' in my child? Is that what he is saying?" I think to myself, shaking my head.

Dr. Dickens continued, "Whilst the chemotherapy drugs wipe out the leukaemia cells, they also wipe out all the good cells as well. Unfortunately, chemical therapy is not very sophisticated and this is why we have to expect that the treatment will cause Emma to be very poorly.

"Do you mean feeling terribly sick?" Louise asks.

"Er, yes, she will feel terribly sick, I'm afraid, but it is the other side effects that are more dangerou..." Dr. Dickens cut himself off, "Problematic," he corrects himself. "Because her good cells are being destroyed, her immune system, amongst other things, will be massively reduced and so she will not be able to fight infections very well. We will have to treat these with antibiotics.

"And, her hair?" I say, rather pathetically, unable to contribute in any other way to this grotesque conversation.

"Well, Vincristine is the drug that makes the hair fall out, but that won't happen for a while yet. All these drugs will be given to Emma orally or by an injection, and because we need to get the drugs directly into her bloodstream, we will need to insert what's called a Hickman line into her chest. We will need to put this line in under general anaesthetic, I'm afraid."

I sigh. I'm thirty-five years old and I've never spent a night in hospital (apart from last night), let alone have an operation under general anaesthetic. My baby's only...well, she's a baby!

Dr. Dickens continued. "There is another medicine that we

have to give Emma every few weeks and to administer this one, we also have to do it under general anaesthetic."

I screw my face up slightly. How much worse is this conversation going to get?

"Yes, you see, we also need to put chemotherapy into her spinal column to make sure the cancer doesn't spread into her brain," he concluded.

Much worse then!

Chapter 11

Halloween: Part Two

It's the 31st October 1977, Halloween. It's Monday, a school night, but that doesn't matter, in fact it is better because everyone will be talking about it in school tomorrow. Me and Tom don't do Halloween in a gang of other mates. We could, but we don't. We just go together. We have our five 'Tricks' ready and carefully laid out on the floor of Tom's bedroom. We have a can of shaving foam, a brown paper bag and the three items that we bought from the joke shop, on our hugely successful Argos outing in Oxford a couple of weeks ago: the Fart Spray, the Stink Bombs and the Devil Bangers.

The Devil Banger experiment turned out to be a massive disappointment. Devil Bangers contain a few grains of gunpowder, individually wrapped in white tissue paper, so that when you throw them at something hard (like the ground or a wall), they go bang. It's not rocket surgery.

Our experiment was to take the Devil Banger concept to the next level. You get about fifty Devil Bangers in a small box that is about twice the size of a box of matches. Each Devil Banger is about half the size of my little finger but each one makes a pretty loud bang. Our experiment was to attempt to make a giant Devil Banger out of the whole box.

We carefully unwrapped each banger and emptied the light grey explosives onto a larger piece of white tissue paper, laid out on the floor of Tom's garage. This took about half an hour but when we had finished we had a sizeable amount of gunpowder. Not enough to blow up the Houses of Parliament, but enough, surely, to scare the shite out of another group of boys out 'Trick or treating.'

Of course, when you are doing this sort of scientific research, you have to carry out a test; remember, if the test was successful, we had two other boxes of Devil Bangers to make a new bomb. So we closed the two mighty doors of the garage at Moss Barn and I carefully pulled all four corners of the tissue paper around the pile of explosive grains, tied the ends with a piece of string and picked up the device; Tom giggled. I had a better chuck than Tom, so I would be the one to set the thing off.

"Ready?" I said.

"Ready." Tom replied taking a step backwards, his green eyes darting about in the gloom of the garage. I hurled the bomb with as much force as I possibly could onto the flagstoned floor. Expecting an ear shattering bang, we both turned our backs and cowed. Nothing. Absolutely nothing. We were expecting a noise that was fifty times the decibels of one Devil Banger, but nothing. The tissue hadn't ripped, so I picked it up again and threw it at the wall. Nothing. I threw it again and again, with a more and more disappointed look on my face each time I chucked it. Nothing. For some reason they must be designed not to go off when you bundle all those high explosives together. How boring.

We shrugged and trudged inside for a biscuit. As we sat on the front steps with our orange squash and digestives, I realised that it was probably a good job that the 'super' Devil

Banger hadn't gone off. If it had ignited, there was so much oil and petrol from Mr Tate's leaky Datsun Sunny on the floor of the garage, the explosion would have taken half of Lambe with us.

Back to Halloween night, the disappointment of the experiment long behind us, we gather up our naughties off Tom's bedroom floor. Tom takes the Fart Spray, a box of four Stink Bombs and a box of Devil Bangers. I grab the shaving foam, my box of stinkies and bangers. We look at the remaining item on the floor. A brown, strong, paper bag about the size of a book. We look at each other seriously. Tom picks up the bag, neatly folds it in half, and half again and puts it in the back pocket of his dark blue jeans.

It's six thirty and it's dark outside. It's been raining but it has stopped now and although it's not very cold we are both wearing jumpers, Parkas and wellies. We don't say goodbye to Mrs Tate, she knows we are off out, it's Halloween isn't it? Jim Tate, Tom's brother, had already gone out to do bad stuff with his mates about half an hour before; we all had tea especially early tonight.

The plan is obviously to get a decent amount of sweets and we know where to go for these: which houses, which people. We're veterans at this. However, "Treats" are not the main reason we are out tonight. We know the addresses of the people who are due some revenge: either the long-term offenders who have upset me or Tom or our families over long periods, or, those who have been recently added to the list because they have committed a crime within the last twelve months. There aren't many of these people in my lovely village, but there are some. And on Halloween, those 'some' have to pay.

We skip out and head towards The Passage to get some easy sugar from the likes of Delia (my mum's best friend and nicest person in the world). We can see the basket of goodies in the window of her small cottage, lit by a pumpkin candle. We politely go through the "Trick or treat?" routine and dive into the basket presented to us. Delia keeps us talking for much too long, but she is too nice to be rude to. So we nod and smile before she closes the door and we run off, out of The Passage, pass The Green and the pub and into Pear Tree Close, where victims number one live.

The Daniels live at number five Pear Tree Close. Their crimes are specifically this:-

1. Edwin Daniels, The Daniels' eleven year old son goes to a private school in Norton. Lambe primary school not good enough for you, Edwin!!!
2. Mr Daniels has a horrible little poodle.

Not horrendous crimes, I admit, but crimes all the same and because justice should fit the crime in any decent society, it will be Fart Spray and Fart Spray only for the Daniels.

Fortunately, we notice that there are a group of four or five children, of similar age to us, just coming down the long drive to number five Pear Tree Close, as we ring the doorbell. We don't recognise them, so they must be from the next village, probably Stonesford, here to take our Lambe sweets from our Lambe families. If we time this just right the comedy will be golden.

Mr Daniels answers the door. Because he took his son off to a private school and we rarely see him (or his son, Edwina) around the village, we know that he won't recognise us.

"Trick or treat?" we demand and he smiles and minces off to the kitchen in his red cardigan, grey slacks and slippers. He comes back with a basket that has some sweets in but also some fruit! We take some Refreshers Chews, thanking him insincerely. He shuts the door and we see him through the window taking the fruit basket back into the kitchen, just as the group of other boys turn up behind us. We push passed them, but hang back a little in the shadows of the trees that line the drive.

"Trick or treat?" We hear the boys ask in ugly Stonesford accents and, as Mr Daniels disappears into the kitchen, we push back passed the boys and Tom lets off a long, reeking volley of Fart Spray from the can, primed and ready in his right hand.

We disappear as quickly as we came along the front of the house, ducking under the large living room window. This all takes only a matter of seconds, so when Mr Daniels returns with his basket, the boys are open mouthed at what they have just witnessed. Mr Daniels, however, has his hand over his nose and is shrieking at the boys, as the stench covers the hall of his house like a thick, stinky, yellow blanket. As me and Tom run down Pear Tree Close and out onto The Green, we can hear the boys protesting as Mr Daniels threatens them with the police; his vile, little poodle yapping around his feet.

Mr Morgan lives at the far end of Stonesford Road on the corner of Cherry Tree Lane. Stonesford Road sits at ninety degrees to Woodstock Street and, as its name suggests, Stonesford Road leads to the next village, the shit heap that is Stonesford, about one mile away.

The road is about two-hundred yards long and is lined either side with modern houses of varying degrees of ugliness. The most unpleasant is reserved for the house where Mr Morgan lives. Made of grey concrete, it is (like the Thatcher's house on The Passage), completely out of place in my Cotswold village. However, having a disagreeable house is not the crime that will warrant Halloween punishment tonight. Oh no. Tonight, revenge will be 'reeked' (literally) on this resident because of something he did and said to my brother six months ago, when my brother rode back from school on his Chopper.

Because Mr Morgan lives on the corner of two roads, it is sometimes unfortunate that boys, of various ages, ride their bikes very close to the small grass verge, outside Mr Morgan's house. It isn't a particularly well kept verge, although on the day this incident took place with my brother, Mr Morgan was out the front doing some gardening on it. I know what happened next because I was only about ten yards behind my brother, on my blue Raleigh Grifter, so I saw and heard what happened very clearly.

As my brother turned left off Stonesford Road and into Cherry Tree Lane, he (ever so slightly), cut the corner and got the back tyre of his Chopper near the grass verge and close to where Mr Morgan was leaning on his spade. Close, seemed to be enough for Morgan, and in a single movement, as my brother whizzed by, Mr Morgan lifted his spade and swung it at full speed, missing my brother's head by a few inches.

My brother jerked his silly shaped handle bars sharp right, narrowly missing a car coming the other way. Clearly disappointed that he hadn't connected his spade with my brother's skull, Morgan yelled out like a mad man, "Go back to Italy, where your ol' man comes from!"

Now, Mr Morgan is younger than my dad, so there is no way that he fought in the Second World War, and therefore can't have any post-traumatic stress relating to fighting Italians. I can, therefore, only assume that he is a bastard.

I followed my brother around the corner, giving the verge and Morgan a wide berth, just in case he fancied collecting me with a rake or something. When we stopped at the end of Cherry Tree Lane and caught our breath, we swore a pact not to tell mum and dad about this but to get Morgan on Halloween, and get him good.

Now, my brother would have normally been out with me and Tom for this particular revenge mission, but he was grounded by mum and dad for something he did on Halloween last year. It was pretty minor; he'd chucked some crab apples at a car's wheels as it went passed The Green. But this is a small village and the owner of the car recognised his coat, stopped the car, gave him a bollocking and told our mum. So let's be clear here, Halloween is not some lawless night where little hooligans are allowed to get away with dreadful behaviour. Not at all. If you get caught doing the bad stuff, you will pay. This is what makes the planning, as well as the execution, so important. Don't get caught.

These words were ringing in my ears as we scooted low across Morgan's front lawn. The lights were on in the front room and upstairs, so we had to be quiet. There would be no, "Trick or treat?" interaction at this front door. The key to this mission was that we knew that Morgan's house had a heavy, spring loaded letterbox. Tom's brother, Jim, does the cancer research lottery collection round every month and had given us the inside information on the letterbox. We waited either side of the front door, like commandos about to storm a building. Our weapons, however, weren't the standard issue M16s with the long barrels, that commandos use. We had bombs, Stinky Bombs.

Making sure Morgan wasn't in the hallway, I gently pushed in the letterbox flap. It was really heavy and needed all my fingers to push it open. As I held the flap, fingers beginning to shake a little with the tension, Tom held a Stink Bomb between his thumb and forefinger of each hand and rested the little glass vials on the bottom lip of the opening. I didn't need to slam shut the flap, I just gently let it drop to allow Tom to remove his fingers. The weight of the spring loaded flap did the rest. A little crack was all that was needed to release the odour from hell, and we quietly crept away back into the gloom of Cherry Tree Lane, avoiding the piles of leaves, with satisfied smiles on our faces.

We didn't need to wait for a reaction from Morgan; it would take a few minutes for the stench to penetrate his living room, but penetrate it would and the smell would last for hours.

We decided to visit some nice people's houses and get some more sweets and gather a few alibis, just in case we needed them. We had one more victim on the list and the best was kept for last.

There is an alleyway that runs from opposite the playing field on Blenheim Road, that (a hundred yards later) comes out in the middle of Woodstock Street. It's a great alley and it gives you access to the back of the hay barns in the far corner of the big farmer's field, that is opposite my house. We go and play in these barns during the summer when it's boiling hot. Whilst the alley gives us great access to the barns, it is, unfortunately, a place where dogs shit. It isn't plagued with dog shit, but if you are ever out to find some, this is the place to be. And tonight, we need some.

We find a decent pile halfway up the alley. I have a torch and Tom removes the brown paper bag from his back pocket, unfolds it and using a piece of wood found nearby, carefully, scoops the muck quickly and efficiently into the bag, as I shine the torch onto this little scene. You would think that Tom has done this before but he hasn't; this is the first time we will be using this particular 'trick.' The brown bag has a sort of plasticky inside to it, so the poo doesn't leak out and once neatly sealed, it doesn't smell.

We pass a few groups of other kids. No one is with a parent, the only adults we see on Halloween are normally in their houses. The groups of kids have their bags of sweets, we have a bag of shite. If the 'super' Devil Banger had worked, now would have been the time to detonate it. Never mind.

We are outside the Thatcher's house now. These are the miseries who constantly moan at my mum and dad for supposedly blocking them in with our car. If they can't get through the massive gap my parents leave them, they shouldn't be driving, simple as that. "You can get a bus through there," my mum is constantly replying to their whinging.

It is a tricky mission this one because the Thatcher's house is in view of my house, and what we are about to do, it will be difficult for my mum and dad not to punish me, if we do get caught. Mr and Mrs Tate won't be best pleased either, particularly as we have already been nabbed chucking snow balls at the Thatcher's front door last winter.

We creep up the pathway and hold our breath as we approach the front door. The Thatchers won't be expecting anyone to knock tonight, all the kids in the village are petrified of them. Tom places the dirty package on the doorstep and takes, from the zipped pocket in the arm of his Parka, a box of Velvet matches, recently purchased (without question) from Bullocks' shop. You can just about see the red and black on the front of the box in the gloom.

These matches are very reliable, there is no wind so the first one lights immediately, and with cupped hands we guide the flame to the corner of the brown paper bag. We wait until the bag is alight and when we know that it won't go out, we both bang on the door as loudly as we can. We sprint out of the pathway and leg it up The Passage at full speed; I trip but Tom grabs me and yanks me forward.

As Mrs Thatcher emerges from the house, she sees a small flaming thing on her doorstep and her immediate reaction (as most people's would be) is to stamp on the conflagration and extinguish the flames. It only takes two stamps of her size seven slippers to put the fire out, but her reward is a sock full of doggy doo. Justice.

We don't stop sprinting until we are almost at the primary school, just by Tom's house. The night's work is complete: just time to squirt half a can of shaving foam on top of the gate posts of the school drive, chuck some Devil Bangers at each other, wish each other good night and head back to our homes; Tom, to hear what pranks and lies his brother has to recall, and me to tell my brother that revenge had been sweet (and smelly).

Chapter 12

It's eight thirty in the evening and I'm trudging up the hill around the back of the hospital, walking passed where I parked the car, badly, the day before. Louise had picked up the car the previous night and parked at the house where I'm heading for now. Clic house.

Clic house is situated, it seems, in a strange part of town high above the city to the north. As I approach the address, the leafy, wide street is lined with large town houses, and the BMWs and Audis in the drives and on the road suggest an affluent area. However, lurking, menacingly, at the top of the street is a large concrete building and a car park that is riddled with graffiti. Not the excellent Banksy art you've learned to expect in Bristol, but the swirly, whirly, colourful but largely artless stuff you see in most city centres.

The contradiction is quite stark and as I pass a pub on the other side of the road, The Hare on The Hill, I can't decide whether it's going to be a snuggly, oak floored free house, serving the south wests' best ales, or a strip lighted, bright, sticky lino floored, cooking lager, shit hole.

As the pub is on the other side of the road, I don't have the energy or the inclination to cross and see what it has to offer. I'm going to need some booze at some point during this horror story, but not tonight.

Clic house is number fifty-three and when I pass number fifty-one, I can see that Clic house is in the same style as all the others. Double fronted, bay windowed, large, one-hundred year old house. I can see our car parked in the tarmacked area outside the house, which would have been gardens years ago. As well as our Ford, there are three other cars in the car park: one big smart Mercedes, a very old battered Renault and a small white van. If these are the vehicles of the parents of cancer kids on ward thirty-four, then it's a good illustration of what Professor Elmwood told me, when I had a quick chat with him before I left the hospital, twenty minutes earlier. "Leukaemia," he had said, "Is indiscriminate. It doesn't matter how old you are, what class you are or how affluent you are, it strikes anywhere."

Louise had been given a key to the front door of Clic house the night before by one of the ward staff. The second key on the small fob is a Yale and that is the key to our bedroom on the first floor. There is no one around, so I have a quick look about downstairs. There's a large sitting room on the left, a surprisingly small kitchen to the right and a big dining room towards the back, which leads to a large garden through some white, plastic framed, French doors. I can see there's a patio with some furniture outside; four green plastic chairs tilted on their front legs, resting against the similarly coloured table. To me, the chairs resemble people with their heads in their hands sitting around a table. It seems very appropriate.

This house is clearly a fantastic amenity, providing a home-from-home exclusively for the parents with kids on ward thirty-four, paediatric oncology, Bristol Children's Hospital. There are a few things that distinguish it from a family home though, including the large amount of neatly filed leaflets in wooden holders dotted about the place. I pick out the first leaflet I see. "Living with Cancer: a parents' guide." I hurriedly shove it back into its slot, not ready yet to come to terms with any of it.

I go up the blandly carpeted stairs to find the door to room two, our room, staring at me when I reach the top. A quick look around informs me that there are probably five bedrooms and a couple of bathrooms up here. It is an enormous house.

I open our door to find a large double bedroom. I sit on the bed and look around. It's spacious: there is a small telly on a desk and a large bay window. It's quite chintzy in décor but comfortable and quiet and I know already that this room will have to be my little place of sanctuary, away from the front line. A place where I will need to recuperate and dress my mental wounds, so that I can go back into battle the next day, and the next.

***

I wake up with a start in the middle of the night. I had obviously fallen asleep on the softish mattress but not under the duvet and I was cold, even though I was fully dressed with my boots still on. I kick them off and as I have no change of clothes, I decide it's worth getting out of my jeans and jumper, so that they aren't too crumpled in the morning, and climb under the duvet, in my pants, socks and T-shirt. I lay on my side and do a 'bicycle kick' movement with my legs that I used to do as a kid, back in Lambe, to get my bed warm. Why was I doing that now, I hadn't done that for twenty-five years?

I must have drifted back off pretty quickly and I woke up around seven thirty the next morning and actually felt I'd had a good night's sleep. I doubted whether Louise and Emma had slept as well. I got up, the curtains weren't drawn and I could see it was going to be a pleasant sunny day. In fact the weather had been lovely and sunny, though cold, for a while and I become instantly annoyed that I will be spending another day in a hospital, devoid of sunlight, when I should be out in the woods with my little boy back in the Forest.

It was then that I realised that actually I wouldn't be kicking leaves around with Alex, because it was Monday and I would normally be driving to London, down the M4 on my way to work on The Old Brompton Road in Chelsea. I'm the HR manager for a charity. A scientific charity. A Cancer Research Charity. Bloody unbelievable isn't it? What are the chances?

I've worked there for about six years and had stayed on even when we had moved to the Forest a year earlier. I was actually working out my three months' notice because I had recently got a similar job at a Council in Gloucester.

I normally drive up on a Monday morning, dead early, down the spectacular Wye Valley, over the beautiful Severn Bridge, then motorway all the way into West London. I would park in the small, exclusive, underground car park beneath our red brick office building on the Old Brompton Road. The car park is normally reserved for the chief executive and the directors, but my boss is lovely and she got me a space. It was a necessity really, because there is nowhere else to park for free in West London on a week day.

I normally stayed up in London with my mate, Jack, until Wednesday. Then I would drive back to the Forest, work from home on Thursday and I had negotiated that I would have Fridays off. It was all pretty perfect in the circumstances, when you consider that work is a hundred-and-twenty miles away from where we live. But I couldn't do it forever, even though I will miss working in London. Anyway, everything's changed now. How am I going to start a new job in two months when my baby's so ill?... That's going to have to be a conversation for another day. Today, however, I will have to call work in London and tell them what's happened.

I had a quick wash in the basin in the corner of the room, that I hadn't noticed last night and brushed my teeth with some water and my finger. I get dressed, sniffing my T-shirt as I do so (I'll need to get some fresh clothes today) and go downstairs. As I open the wide, stained glass windowed front door, I meet a couple, slightly younger than me both in their late twenties/early thirties, coming into Clic house. The man has his arm tightly wrapped around the woman, who has her head down and is clearly upset. The husband and I acknowledge each other with a half-smile and we slip, silently, passed each other. Who knows what stage they are at in their perilous journey?

This is only the second time I've entered the hospital. I decide to take the stairs rather than deal with Wallace's cheery ways in the lift. I may as well do some exercise, as I will be sat on my arse for the next twelve hours, twelve days, twelve weeks, twelve whatevers. The stairwell I take winds up the front of the building and I notice that the windows on each floor are at waist level. A brilliant and simple design but it reminds me, sadly, that the main occupants of this hospital are about three feet tall. I do feel a bit better though, telling myself that many hospitals (including the Cancer Hospital that is attached to my place of work in London) are very old, Victorian and worn out. Bristol Children's Hospital, on the other hand, is pretty much brand spanking new.

My relative good mood is short lived. Louise looks as exhausted as I felt twenty-four hours earlier. Never the most patient or natural mother, Louise is clearly relieved to see me and is already gathering her things together, like a night worker about to be relieved by the next shift.

"How has she been?" I ask Louise but looking at Emma half asleep.

"Terrible night," she replies. "She pulled her cannula out of her hand, so the nurse had to put it in again, but she couldn't find a vein. It took about an hour in the end." Emma's cannula was again attached to a drip on the machine that whirred and whooshed at regular intervals. I gave Emma a light kiss on the forehead that didn't seem to register at all.

"Has Professor Elmwood been around yet?" I ask, looking around the ward.

"No," replies Louise.

"I need to phone work today and sort that out but I'll wait 'til we've seen the doctor," I mumble.

I go to get two coffees from the machine and as I'm fumbling for some change, Professor Elmwood and a gaggle of male and female junior doctors sweep by deep in conversation, ignoring the stressed dad attempting to put lids on boiling hot cups of weak, watery, brownness.

When I return, the pack of doctors are around Emma's bed (we were bed one, after all). A pretty, long brown haired, junior doctor pulls the curtain around the bed with one hand; the other hand is holding a file.

Professor Elmwood sits on the bed next to Emma and smiles at Louise and myself and asks how we are doing. We give a 'worn out' kind of shrug. Emma's top has ridden up, high above her swollen tummy and the Professor gently feels her stomach, then her glands and has a quick look in her eyes, whilst she wriggles and moans.

"So," he said, "We have already started her on her chemotherapy last night. We have to dissolve the tablets in a syringe with water and try and give her these orally. I understand from the nurse it didn't go very well last night and she spat it out." I looked at Louise and she nodded. "So, we will have to put a tube into her nose that goes down her throat and into her stomach. It isn't very nice I'm afraid but it does mean that she won't taste any of the drugs, and we need to get as much of the medicine into her as possible.

We need to ensure that remission happens quickly."

I guess I'm looking a bit confused, so he explains. "One of the success factors in fighting A.L.L is that the cancer currently in Emma, is eradicated very quickly. So it is essential that she keeps down as much of the medicine as possible. One of the nurses will put the tube down this morning. It isn't very nice to watch, so please don't feel you have to be here when they do it."

Great opportunity to demonstrate my cowardice, I think to myself. "I think we would rather be with her," I lied.

"That's fine," he said. "The nurse will let you know before they do it." I nod, feeling slightly sick. I'm not squeamish, it's just that I don't like seeing little children in great pain or discomfort, which I guess is reasonable. "I'll be back tomorrow morning," the Professor concludes, coughing slightly as he stood up, looking a little pale himself today. He's probably as exhausted as the rest of us, I thought, but still having to make life saving decisions every five minutes.

The doctors leave and I go to make the phone call to work. I feel I need complete privacy, so I leave the hospital out of the front and through the undercover ambulance bay, where Emma had been dropped off two days earlier. I walk out into the sunshine (it is actually quite warm for March), turn left, head down the busy high street for some twenty metres, cross the road and walk down a side street opposite the eye hospital. There, I sit on a step that looks like an old side entrance to the Victorian hospital, bring up my work number, press the green 'call' button, and take a deep breath.

Amanda Watts, my friend and colleague, answered the phone. She isn't my boss now, but she used to be when I first started working with her six years ago.

"Hi," she says. I just break down. I can't get the words out; I haven't told anyone about Emma except my parents. I haven't even spoken to my brother yet, mum and dad had told him. "Oh my God," Amanda said, "What's happened?"

I sorted myself out enough to tell her the horrible truth of the last two days. It was her turn to be speechless. You see, we all work for a scientific cancer research charity; we use the 'C' word all day, everyday, even us administration knobbers. One of the departments I actually support is leukaemia research; Professor Merv Green (who is in charge of it) and I sit down together and regularly interview postdoctoral scientists for jobs in his laboratory. But the words 'cancer' and 'leukaemia' are just words to an HR manager like me. They aren't real, it doesn't happen to anyone I know. None of our friends or the people I work with, including the scientific staff (there are about eight-hundred of them) has a child who has leukaemia. I know this, because someone would have said so. It's that rare.

Amanda reassures me that all my work will be picked up, I mustn't come back in and that she will talk to Karen, our boss, and explain everything. I thank her, press the red 'end call' button, put my head in my hands and sob, again.

Chapter 13

Neil

My brother's called Neil Alessandro. My dad chose his middle name (actually he chose both my brother's names – Mum said, after giving birth to him, she didn't care what he was called. He took ages apparently). He was born on 19th November 1966, so he is a year and a half older than me and a school year above me.

I love my brother. He quite likes me, but I guess it's an older brother's job not to be too nice to his younger sibling. We get on pretty well though, really.

This morning, my brother is kneeling down on a green cushion, dressed in a white cotton smock, with a frilly red collar tight around his eleven year old neck. He has his school shoes on but it's a Sunday. He is an altar boy in the eleventh Century St. Sebastian Church of England Church, in Lambe; which is about a minute's walk from our house. He is trying so hard to stop laughing his face has gone red and it looks like his head might explode. I know this because I am kneeling on a similar cushion, in a similarly ridiculous dress on the other side of the altar. "The Body of Christ. The Blood of Christ. The Body of Christ. The Blood of Christ," Mr Thomas the vicar, drones on and on, as he feeds and waters (or is it wines?) the small congregation lined up in the freezing cold house of God.

For some reason, when the Vicar had asked my mum, last week, if me and Neil would be altar boys, she didn't hesitate in saying, "Yes."

My parents don't believe in God, as far as I know, and they very rarely go to church (although we have been to the occasional midnight mass on Christmas Eve and of course primary school stuff). So why she thought it was a good idea for me and Neil to do churchy stuff was beyond us.

Neil was more cross with mum than I was, and I was furious. Neil normally goes fishing on Sunday mornings and I sometimes go with him. Church at 10am was not the place to be. Mum and dad had both said that they would come and see us 'book-ending' the altar; I noticed, however, as I turned my head and stared across the surprisingly full church, that my normally very reliable parents, hadn't managed to make the one-hundred paces from their front door to the church, on this wet and windy November morning.

I peer around the altar again to check that Neil hasn't actually exploded. He hasn't, but now he seems to be getting slightly distressed. His face is even redder and he is coughing. It turns out that as he was preparing the 'Body of Christ' and putting the two pence sized discs of bread onto the gold plate (that Mr Thomas, the vicar, was holding), he'd managed to slip five of them into his month without Mr Thomas noticing.

Now, if just one of these discs of bread/cardboard, which are fed to the parishioners, gets stuck to your palate, you need a chisel and a bucket of water to dislodge it. If you get five stuck up there, you are going to choke and then die.

"Body of Christ. The Blood of Chri…" as Mr Thomas fed

the last woman in the line (it was Mrs Hampton-Brown from the big house with the tennis court), Neil coughed one last time and a soggy ball, the texture of putty, flew out of his gob and landed about a pace behind the vicar's left foot. No one else saw it because they had their heads bowed in prayer. What me and Neil saw, however, was Mr Thomas take a small step backwards in his shiny, creaky, black leather shoes and stand on the gross, sticky deposit.

Now, I know it would have been funnier if he had slipped on the bread and thrown the 'Blood of Christ' (the wine in the gold goblet that he was holding) all over himself. But this is real life and that didn't happen. However, it was enough that he had stepped on the mushy blob to make me and Neil burst into laughter.

As the good Lambe folk filed back to their pews, Mr Thomas turned and gave us a disapproving look. He was a boring vicar but he was a decent chap, and I was sure this wouldn't go further than the three of us. I was wrong. He told mum and as a punishment we would have to deliver the parish newsletter to all the houses up The Passage, every Sunday evening for the rest of our lives. However, we were never asked to be altar boys again, so our punishment was taken with good grace.

Me and Neil have got a snooker table. We got it last Christmas. It doesn't have its own legs, so it sits on the dining room table. We normally eat in the kitchen, so the snooker table has stayed up most of the year; unless my mum and dad are having a dinner party or something with their friends. In these circumstances the 'green baize' is taken from the dining table and put behind our large, red Chesterfield sofa. The table is six feet by four feet and is made from chip board (not slate, like the ones in the Crucible at the World Championships, or the one on Pot Black).

It is early Sunday evening and me and Neil are in the ninth frame of a very serious game, which has carried on all weekend. It's four frames all and thirty-five to twenty-eight points to me in the deciding frame. We don't play for prize money or glory. We play for dead legs. The loser of the game will be required to stand, leaning against the dining room wall, with a straight leg, whilst the winner, the victor, has one opportunity, and one only, to inflict a dead leg onto his opponent.

Dead legs are caused when the knee is brought in at speed to the victim's thigh, sending him sprawling to the ground in agony. There is an art to dead legging, and I am bloody good at it. You have to catch the thigh exactly in the right place. Half an inch either side and the knee slips off the target and your quarry gets away with only mild pain and a small bruise. Get it right, and the buggers not getting up until teatime. Still, I will be the one getting crippled by Neil if I don't pot this final pink and black.

We are both quite good at snooker, but not brilliant. My best break ever is twenty-seven, and it is rare if we pot more than five balls in a row. However, I am confident about my chances this evening. The pink is on its spot and I've got a straight pot into the bottom left-hand corner pocket. The black is over the right middle pocket and an easy pot, so if the pink does go down, it's game over and curtains for Neil's

Fran Gabaldoni

leg.

I chalk up the cue and pop the square block back into my waistcoat pocket. Oh yes, I forgot to say, we are both wearing dad's old waistcoats. Mine is a green velvet (not sure why dad bought it or where he wore it), Neil's is black. They are obviously much too big for us but you have to wear them, it's in the rules.

I line up the pot; it is so straight it's going to need a bit of 'stun' on it to stop the white ball following the pink ball into the pocket, and giving Neil a six point 'foul' and basically handing him the match. So I place the tip of the cue at the base of the white ball, look up to see Neil biting his lip and holding his breath, focus back on the white ball and strike it.

It's as clean as a whistle: white ball stops dead, pink sinks in the corner without even 'wiping its feet' on the jaws of the pocket. "Oh shit!" I hear Neil exhale. I give him a little smile and even though I don't need to pot the black ball, I do so with cocky ease.

Now this sort of punishment may seem a little weird: two medium sized boys, both under twelve, dressed in waistcoats, causing serious (though not lasting) injuries to each other over a game of snooker. You might be right, but it still makes us laugh. Anyway, we both entered the nine framed game knowing the consequences. No one has been tricked here. We never play our friends for dead legs, it's just a brother thing.

Anyway, Neil took his dead leg on the chin, as it were. He went straight down, but I didn't quite catch him right and he was up again within forty-five minutes.

We like playing snooker me and Neil, but what we really love is playing cricket up the drive at our house. We don't play cricket for dead legs though, we play so that one day we can play for England in a test match. We play all year round, it isn't just a summer sport for us. There would have to be snow on the ground for us not to play, and even then we might get a game in.

Our drive isn't very long, it has a garage at the end of it attached to the kitchen. That's where the batsman stands. When the bowler runs in, he can see the three windows of the kitchen on the left, the batsman, and then the garage door to the right. The drive is lined by a dry stone wall on the right, and the side of the house on the left.

Our drive is nearly perfectly designed for two small boys to play cricket on, because the ball can't go very far and you don't waste hours chasing it. A glorious cover drive or a square cut will come to rest shortly after striking the wall of the house. A pull, hook or clip off the legs will hit the dry stone wall. The wicketkeeper is the garage door and the slips are the kitchen windows. Oh yeah, and that's why I said the drive is only nearly perfect for playing cricket. Those windows can be a problem.

The only time you really end up chasing the ball, if you are the bowler, is when the batsman hits the ball straight back over the bowlers head – where it will go down the road, down the hill and won't stop until it gets to the playing field two-hundred yards away.

Me and my brother play cricket for hours up this drive. I am a better batsman than Neil, but he is a better bowler, so our contests are pretty even. He probably gives up and goes in a little sooner than me though, normally complaining of a S.A or sweaty arse. Although mum lets us play cricket up the drive (and normally leaves her car down on the bottom bit so we have enough room to play), she always says, "Don't hit the windows." When dad gets home from work and sees us playing cricket up the drive, he also kindly leaves his car down on the bottom bit behind mums, but he always says, "Watch those windows."

The drive is made from concrete and is pretty smooth but it does have a few cracks in it, just outside the line of where the off stump would be if you are a right handed batsman (like me and Neil both are). We don't use proper stumps though, just an old board from out of the garage. The cracks can give the bowler some good assistance if the ball lands in them; forcing the batsman to play a false shot, the ball hits the edge of the bat and you can regularly get caught out by the pretend slip fielders, or, 'the windows,' as my mum and dad rightly call them!

It's June 1978. Saturday morning. Sunny and already hot. Over the spring, mum and dad have had a small extension put on the back of the kitchen. The extension and bigger kitchen are all very nice but, more importantly, it hasn't affected our ability to play cricket up the drive. The only thing that's changed are the brand spanking new kitchen windows. Now, if the batsman does 'edge' the tennis ball, which we play with, and it flies towards the windows, it does so at a pretty slow speed and would never actually smash a window. We know this because we have hit them on many occasions without mum and dad knowing. So we are not worried about these new windows when we head out at eleven o'clock to start our test match.

England are playing Pakistan at Edgbaston in Birmingham today and I have a new batting hero. A lanky, left handed, blond, curly haired chap who plays for Leicestershire and he is making his debut for England in this match. His name is David Gower and I intend to be playing cricket with him for England in nine years' time, when I am nineteen years old.

Neil has won the toss and elected to bat. I will be coming in off my long run, because I am a fresh and fit ten year old. I've got my cut off denim shorts on, a T-shirt and black Adidas trainers. Neil is wearing thick brown corduroy trousers which, I know, is a mistake because it is so warm. I already have the upper hand in the contest; in an hour's time Neil will be trudging off to the toilet complaining of a S.A.

Unfortunately, we don't play for an hour today. In fact, we don't even play for one minute. We play for one ball. As I come in off my long run, revved up and over excited, I get to my delivery stride and complete a terrible bowling action that sends the green Dunlop tennis ball two yards wide of my batting brother, directly through one of the new kitchen window panes.

There is stunned silence. This has never happened before. In a million deliveries, neither of us have bowled a ball so badly, so violently off course, that it would hit the windows without even bouncing. We simply hadn't counted for it. This was a disaster. An unmitigated disaster for two reasons:-

a) The parent bollocking would be monumental

b) It had ruined the day's cricket.

"You prick!" Is Neil's first contribution to resolving this situation. His second, however, is genius, pure genius. Sitting, discarded in the garage are the old rotten window frames the builders had removed and had yet to cart away. But how many panes were left in them? I know they had broken one when they took it out, because I remember seeing them sweeping up the glass when I came home from school a few weeks ago. Neil drops the bat, opens the garage doors and I can tell by the look on his face that there is unbroken glass in the frame.

We both drag the window carcass, carefully, out of the garage and lean it against the wall. There is one pane of glass left in the middle section. It is splattered with a bit of paint and it's dusty. It's about three feet high by two feet wide and exactly the same size as the one I've just smashed. If we can remove the broken pane, gently take out the replacement one and get it in place by one o'clock (when mum and dad will be back from their Saturday food shopping trip in Witney), we may yet live. We can do this. Only just, but we can do it.

***

It's twelve thirty. Parent ETA: Thirty minutes. Operation: 'Save My Stupid Life' has gone without a hitch so far. My duties are menial: tidying up the broken glass in the kitchen and on the drive, removing the broken glass from the window pane and looking for the tennis ball.

"Found it!" I shout, removing the ball from behind the pine dresser in the kitchen.

"Tosser." I hear Neil reply, as he gently, gently taps the tiny nails he had found in dad's toolbox, into the wooden frame to hold the new (well old, actually) window pane in place. Neil is much more practical than me, mending our bikes and stuff. All he needs to do once the nails are in place is to putty around the edge of the window, clean the glass and then, Mission: 'I'm an Arsehole/Neil's a Life Saver' will be complete. The putty had been left by the builders so that's no problem, and the new window frame hadn't been painted yet anyway, so Neil's fix wouldn't be noticed by mum or dad.

I come out of the kitchen with the ball in my hand and ask how he was getting on. "OK," he says, "nearly done." He is stood on an upturned crate, with a hammer in his right hand and a nail between his lips, like a professional. "How long have we got?" He asks out of the corner of his mouth, careful not to drop the nail. I look at my Casio digital watch.

"About ten minutes, I reckon." I reply, beginning to feel slightly more relaxed. We were going to get away with this, we really were.

Neil took the nail from his mouth, placed it in the final space in the bottom left-hand corner of the frame, tapped it in position and… crack. Not a big noise, just a gentle crack. The noise my guts made falling out of my arse was considerably louder.

The split in the glass covered about half the pane. We had failed, right at the last. Neil climbed off the crate, let the hammer drop down by his side, took a deep breath, but didn't say anything. Dad's blue Lancia Beta Coupe 2000 swung around off the road and into the drive.

Of course we got a bollocking, wouldn't any kids in this situation? Mum and dad weren't severe though, they never were really. I took most of the blame and I think mum and dad were both quietly quite proud of what Neil, their eleven year old (about to go off to big school next term) had nearly accomplished. I know I was, though I would never tell him. Perhaps we'll give cricket up for a couple of weeks anyway, because the Football World Cup has just started in Argentina!

Chapter 14

I put my mobile back in my pocket and start to wander back to the hospital in a bit of a daze. At least I had sorted work out, so that was some pressure off. When I got onto the ward, I steered myself to bed one. When I got there the bed was empty, with no sheets on it. Louise was looking over Emma, who was in a small cot, so pale and writhing around.

An overweight, middle aged woman in a pinkish uniform arrived with new bed sheets.

"What's happened?" I ask Louise.

"An explosive poo!" she said holding her nose. "Really bad, like I've never seen before," she continued. I could smell a faint, whiffy odour still lingering in the air. "They think it's the medicine," she concluded.

I had a quick look around the ward. No one new had been brought in, but bed six was empty, and there was none of the medical or personal paraphernalia around the bed that indicates that it has an occupant.

"Wonder what happened to them?" I ask Louise, not remembering who was in bed six yesterday.

"They got moved to a side room," she replied. That was a happier outcome than I had grimly anticipated and hoped that shortly we would be in a side room and off this ward with its noise, the loud tellies and the lack of privacy. I'm staying with Emma tonight on the ward and I'm not looking forward to it.

It's still Monday, only day three, although it feels like a lifetime already. It's four o'clock in the afternoon and Dr. Jim Dickens has just paid us a visit. He's a bit worried about Emma's diarrhoea, which has got worse throughout the day, and has requested that a sample be checked in microbiology. He's not sure if it is just the medicine making her this bad. He is concerned about how dehydrated she is becoming from the diarrhoea and how little she is drinking and eating; so he has decided that the feeding tube is to go in tonight (great, that's on my shift then, I'm looking forward to that!). He also needs to get her tummy x-rayed because it is terribly bloated now. She looks, to me, like an Ethiopian famine victim, but in negative.

Emma's slot for an x-ray finally arrives and a cheery porter goes around all four corners of the bed, taking the brakes off the wheels with his foot. The radiography technician introduces herself but I forget her name instantly; she checks the details on Emma's wrist band against a form on a clipboard. When she has done her checks she places the clipboard on the bed and between them the technician and the porter, competently, wheel the bed out of the ward and into a big lift. Louise and I follow.

***

We're back on the ward, the results of the x-ray will be with the doctor for the morning round. I feel I want the answers from the x-ray immediately but that's only because I'm anticipating more bad news. Louise leaves at about eight thirty in the evening for Clic house, and the chance of a reasonable night's sleep. Shortly after she has gone, a nurse called Kate, arrives to put Emma's feeding tube in. I say that I will stay, but this nurse takes control of the situation and advises me that the first time is not the nicest to watch; she always recommends that parents go off, have a coffee and when they come back, it is all done. I don't need a second invitation to miss this little show, so I thank her, give Emma a kiss and skulk out of the ward, down to the restaurant, which is almost empty, and get a coke from the machine and sit down at a table.

When I return twenty minutes later, I find Emma awake, with a thick yellow tube disappearing down her right nostril. I'm not sure where it's gone, but I assume it's down in her bloated little tum. On the other end of the tube is what looks like a valve with a plastic cap, where I guess drugs and liquids will get flushed into her. There is a big bit of clear tape on her cheek to hold the tube in position. I look at my sick little girl. How did this happen?

***

It's six thirty, Tuesday morning and I've just survived my second night on the ward. It was awful, even worse than the first. As a result I've probably had an hour's sleep at best. The night goes something like this:-

9pm: Observations for temperature, pulse and blood pressure.

10pm: Bloods taken for analysis.

12 midnight: Drugs syringed down her new nose tube for the first time.

1.30am: A drip is attempted to be attached to the cannula on her hand.

1.45am: Drip not working. Machine alarming, beeping and flashing the word 'Occlusion!' Which apparently means blockage.

2.15am: Nurse puts in a new cannula into Emma's other hand, to her discomfort.

2.45am: New drip is attached, which seems to work.

3am: No it doesn't. Machine alarm sounding again, 'Occlusion!' flashing. Cannula flushed and checked, seems OK; apparently Emma just lying on the line and blocking the flow.

3.30am: Change nappy, huge, stinking poo.

4am: Observations.

6am: Meds given, bloods taken.

6.30am: Dad knackered. Emma asleep.

Chapter 15

World Cup

"Bettega! Rossi! Bettega! Bettega! One-nil!" This is the commentary to the beautifully fluid, one-two move between the Italian international football stars, Roberto Bettega and Paolo Rossi, as they go one-nil up against the 1978 World Cup hosts, Argentina. Me and Neil are going wild.

When Mr Morgan tried to behead my brother with his spade, way back last year, you may remember that he shouted out (as he swung his weapon), "Go back to Italy, where your ol' man comes from!" Well, the old fool did get his geography right, at least. My dad is from Italy and he is Italian, making me and my brother, Neil, half Italian (actually, it's a bit less than half, but it's complicated...).

I am, therefore, a massive Italian football fan and I will always support Italy over England. England are rubbish and haven't even qualified for this, most amazing, of World Cup tournaments in South America. That's good, because I don't have to take any stick off my friends who support England. Anyway, because England aren't there, for some reason all the boys are suddenly Holland supporters, attempting, very badly, to pronounce Dutch names in strong West Oxfordshire accents.

Even my best friend, Tom, thinks I should support England because I live here. However, it is the only thing we have ever disagreed on. My mum's English (actually, she is half English/half welsh, which isn't complicated). She would be supporting England, but because the English players are back at home in their mock Tudor houses, in Essex and Liverpool, and not in Buenos Aires, she is an honorary

Italian for the next few weeks.

This is the first World Cup that I can remember. I might have seen some of the stuff in Germany four years ago, but I would only have been six, or something. This is the first time I have seen such important matches on the telly, with players on show like Claudio Gentile, Franco Causio and Dino Zoff; and then pretend to be them, down at the playing field, where ten or twelve other boys would be gathered to play football until it is too dark to see the ball.

In Bullocks' shop, me and Tom are spending all our pocket money on ALL-STAR crisps (well, they're not crisps actually, they are more of a corn snack, I would say). Inside the packets are football cards, with drawings of the World Cup heroes we have been watching. We don't have a sticker book, just merrily collect as many as we can. Tom kindly gave me Paolo Rossi yesterday, who he found in his packet of salt 'n' vinegar. I disappointedly ended up with a player from Iran who I had never heard of.

Italy are having a good tournament so far, progressing through the first group stage. Dad has put a World Cup chart up on the wall in the kitchen by the side of the cooker. He doesn't like, or follow, first division or club football in the slightest, but like me, he loves the World Cup. Dad, religiously, fills in the chart when he gets home from work. Taking a pen from his suit pocket or out of his brief case, he carefully fills in the scores and writes in the teams that have made it through to the next round. The wall chart has a streak of olive oil right down the middle of it, and although the chart is getting messy, its position in the kitchen allows dad to study the chart, while he cooks up delicious pasta sauces.

I do quite like first division football and I might watch Match of the Day on a Saturday evening and On the Ball or Football Focus on Saturday lunchtimes. However, until this year, I was never sure which first division club to support. I never really liked Liverpool, Manchester United or Arsenal (Neil's team); everyone supported these three. It wasn't until me, Neil, mum and dad happened to be in Wembley high street this May, on the day of the 1978 FA cup final. My dad had just got a job in Wembley and for some reason, the day he chose to take us up there to see his office, was the busiest day in Wembley's calendar.

The final was between the mighty Arsenal and the massive underdogs, Ipswich Town. As we were walking up the road, a huge group of red supporters were coming towards us; menacingly chanting Arsenal fans. Going the other way, walking just ahead of us, was a single, blue shirted Ipswich fan, who, without hesitation, aggression or seeking a fight, walked straight through the Arsenal clan. Astonishingly, the sea of red parted and he made it through, without any hassle. I was, from that point on, an Ipswich Town fan. I have no idea what part of the country they come from, but who cares.

Of course, Ipswich, went on to win the final, one-nil, with a goal from Roger Osborne and so I was happy (I was always happy) that I had made a good choice. I wonder if they will ever win it again?

The days are long and sunny and the international football matches from a sultry, exotic place, fills our TV screens all afternoon. We then go and play down the field until we can run about no longer, go home and watch the evening games. Dad lets us stay up late. Skinny, long haired superstars in light blue and white striped shirts and tiny little black shorts, send their fans wild by getting to the final of their home tournament. Argentina have overcome their early defeat by my Italy and beat the Brazilians in the semi-final.

The other semi-final is between Italy and Holland. All the boys from school who had initially supported Holland, typically stopped supporting them when the Dutch were beaten by Scotland in a brilliant, but ultimately irrelevant game. An old Scotsman with a bald head danced around the orange defenders and scored, but it wasn't enough. Scotland went home and Holland, eventually, got through to the semi-final; where they ended up beating the Italians with some unbelievable, curling, long range shooting.

I was disappointed when the handsome men in azzurri blue trudged off the field as losers in the semi-final. Some of them look a bit like my dad in photographs I've seen of him when he was younger. But I didn't stay sad for long. I never do.

In our games down the park we tried to replicate the brilliant, long range goals from near the halfway line, but we can't even reach the eighteen yard box. Me and Tom reckoned that our legs would break if we tried to hit the ball that hard.

In Argentina, Mario Kempes breaks the Dutch hearts and Holland lose another World Cup final. Ticker tape pours onto the pitch. Magnificent!

Chapter 16

It's nine thirty in the morning, still Tuesday, day four. Professor Elmwood is towering over Emma, who is awake and moaning quietly. I'm sat in the light blue, plastic coated, high backed chair by the side of the bed that is relatively comfortable. Louise is sat on the side of the bed. The curtains are drawn and there are a couple of junior doctors that were here yesterday and that I have seen on the ward now many times.

The kind Professor opens with, "We are still awaiting the x-ray results on Emma's tummy from last night." I immediately felt frustration and disappointment that there was a delay. "It should be with us shortly. Actually, can you chase that up now, please?" He turned to one of the juniors, who quietly slipped out of the curtain to carry out the request. "Our concern this morning," he continued, "is Emma's diarrhoea." We have the test back from microbiology and I'm afraid to say that she has contracted Norwalk."

Louise and I looked at each other, confused and then back at the consultant. "I'm afraid the Norwalk infection has been contracted since she has been in hospital. It's not directly linked to the cancer, although her condition will not be helping her," he said. I sigh, audibly.

"Do you mean she has caught something on the ward?" I say, with a slightly annoyed tone.

"I'm afraid so," Professor Elmwood replied. "Norwalk is a bug that can make you very unwell, and cause chronic diarrhoea as we are seeing in Emma now. It means that we need to get a large amount of fluid into her, so we will increase her saline drip." A junior doctor scribbles on a chart. "What we really need to do, is to get this Hickman line in. That's the one that goes into her chest, so that antibiotics and the medicines can go straight into her bloodstream. The problem we have, is I don't really want to do that procedure whilst she has this Norwalk virus. You may remember she will have to have the procedure under general anaesthetic."

I can feel my lips pursing and my hands tighten slightly on the handles of the chair. The Professor continues, "The most important thing to do today, however, is to get you all into a side room." I loosen my grip on the chair and relax my face a little. "Because Norwalk is highly infectious, she will need to be 'barrier' nursed in the side room. This means that the strictest hygiene procedures will need to apply when people enter the room."

I envisage medical personnel in white, hooded boiler suits, with thick, green rubbers gloves and masks tending to my daughter, who is just in a nappy. Professor Elmwood acknowledges my concerned face and says, "It basically means all hospital staff will wear plastic aprons and gloves when they tend to Emma." I was right then!

"Ok," I respond. "How unwell will she be?"

"Very, I'm afraid. It is an unpleasant virus, and with everything else, she will be quite poorly. We will try and sort the room out by this afternoon, and get you all a bit more comfortable."

The morning dragged on. Nurses carried out observations every few hours, Louise, calm as ever, sits and reads Heat magazine in the blue chair. I fidget, restless, exhausted, perched on the bed. The sides of the bed, that protect Emma from rolling out, are down. They are pretty much redundant anyway, as she doesn't seem to have the energy to roll onto her side, let alone wriggle across the acres of white cotton and fall out onto the floor.

I notice the small, brown bruises all over her body, arms and legs. They are the only colour she has apart from white. Her lips have no pink in them at all. A lifeless colour almost. Her beautiful, piercing blue eyes are shadowed behind their thin lids; her tummy still swollen. No news on that yet. Since Professor Elmwood's visit this morning, I've already asked various passing doctors if the results from the x-ray are back yet. They check at the desk and come back with a negative reply.

It's just after four o'clock in the afternoon, the ward is noisy and busy. I had been out shopping for an hour and a half. I'd bought some essentials: some socks and pants, toiletries, a couple of T-shirts and a coat. I had needed a new one anyway and found something nice in an independent shop on Park Street. When I was out, I had phoned mum and dad, who are still staying at our house to look after Alex. He was at school, so I didn't get to speak with him. Mum and dad are super concerned, I can tell, but they are trying to be positive. Already, it feels like a chore to recount what is happening on ward thirty-four to my mum and dad and Louise's parents; but they need to hear what's going on just as much as Louise and I do. In some ways it is harder for them because they are an hour away, waiting for twice daily updates.

I'm disappointed I couldn't speak to Alex. I had lost track of time and hadn't realised he was still at school. I asked mum how he was. I could tell by her slightly delayed response that he was missing us, but she thoughtfully played it down. I could see right through it though and said I would call later and speak to him. I was really missing him. He's a worrier. I had picked that up already in his short three and a half years' of life so far. Louise suffers from depression and I feel I can already see some of her traits in little Alex. Or, is that just me being the worrier? Hell, I've got enough on my plate to concern myself with, without worrying about my son's mental health at the moment. "Bloody man up, will you!" I scream to myself. But I'm exhausted, I know I am, emotionally and physically. I need some good news, just something little, something to boost me slightly. It doesn't come.

"I'm sorry, but the side room won't be available until tomorrow now." Dr. Jim Dickens apologies. A nurse is also present, gently tending to Emma, taking her temperature and blood pressure for the millionth time. Emma whimpers and then cries as she fouls her nappy again.

It's early evening and Louise and I are in the hospital canteen, picking our way through something that looks like Lasagna. "Alex was a bit upset on the phone," I said. I had called him just before we came off the ward. "Oh, love him," was her rather irritatingly relaxed reply. I didn't say anything else, it wasn't the time for a row, caused by me just because I'm shattered. Louise is going through the same as I am, she just deals with it very differently.

She's struggled badly looking after the children, ever since they were born really. Neither of the kids were breast fed (Louise's antidepressants were a factor) and I did my fair share of night bottle feeding and nappy changing, even when I was working the next day, so that Louise didn't get too tired.

I guess it has been hard for Louise with the kids during the working week for the past few months, because I spend two nights away in London. But it was mainly her idea to move to the country before I had secured a job nearer to home. I always felt I had another couple of years' of London life left in me, but I guess the flat was quite small and Louise had started climbing the walls.

I was just beginning to sense, as I put my fork down on my half eaten 'pasta,' that Louise was already enjoying having me here to help out with Emma twenty-four hours a day and not being at work, even in these terrible circumstances. She needed me, just as much as Emma did. Unfortunately, and unbeknown to Louise, I had, over the past few months, been thinking that I wasn't very happy in our marriage. I didn't want to think like this, I really didn't. But I was. Christ, I would have to put those thoughts to one side now.

It was raining, steadily, as I walked up the hill towards Clic house, later that evening. The cosy lights in The Hare on the Hill pub beckoned to me through the swirling rain. I pulled the big collar up on my new, woolen, double breasted, black coat and walked on by. I still felt that I didn't deserve a pint yet.

Chapter 17

School trip

It's the day of the school trip. But this is no ordinary school trip. This isn't a day trip to the Cotswold wildlife park, or the Ashmolean museum with the shrunken heads. Oh no. This is a five day school trip to the middle of Wales, or somewhere. No mum or dad, no brother. Just me, Tom, five other boys and two teachers. Oh yeah, and some girls.

It's the middle of October 1978, and it's mine, Tom's and everyone else in my class' last year of primary school. Actually, it's not everyone's last year in my class. Lambe primary school has only about sixty kids; it's tiny. There are only three classes, so there are two school years in each class. I am in my final year but half the class are a year younger. None of the younger ones are on this school trip.

We get to school at seven o'clock in the morning, it's Saturday. The light grey minibus awaits us on the school playground. Mr Walker (or Whip Wap Walker as he is known to us, for no particular reason), the Headmaster, is loading bags onto the fifteen seater Leyland. Just before we set off, my mum gets out her Polaroid camera and takes a snap of me and Tom, dressed in our Parka coats, standing by the open side door of the bus. We jump in, middle seats, Tom by the window on the right-hand side. We are all chattering quietly, you can sense the immense excitement amongst everyone. We will need to stop the bus for wee-wees about every twenty minutes at this rate.

Stephen Roberts is late, but once he bundles in, Mr Walker slams the door shut, jumps into the driver's seat, reverses down the drive and we all wave to our mums and dads and head off in the direction of Stoneford, the next village, and then on towards Witney, the nearest town. After that, I will have absolutely no idea where we are, or where we are going, until we get there.

The journey is long, but fun. I have no idea how long it has taken, but we stopped for sandwiches just before we crossed a massive white bridge, going over a massive brown river leading into a massive, brown, swirling sea. Motorways turn into main roads that turn into smaller, narrower roads, until we arrive at our destination down a single track, lined by high, dry stone walls.

There are sheep in the green, green, fields either side of the track and some in the track itself. Mr Walker toots the horn for them to move, then stops for Mrs Webster (the only other grown-up on the bus) to open a five bar metal gate. Mr Walker swings through the gate, stops again for Mrs Webster to climb in and then heads, slowly down the narrow, long drive, covered in moss, towards what looks like an old farm house. Boney M's 'Brown Girl in the Ring,' is playing on the minibus radio.

***

It's four days later and I am stood by the edge of the most beautiful, clear blue pool of water. The pool is about as big as our school playing field and is surrounded by steep sides of dark grey. We are in an old slate mining quarry, and it is absolutely amazing, and I mean absolutely amazing! It is skimming heaven. I am good at skimming; I've got quite a good arm on me because of all the cricket I play up the drive and on the school field. Me and Neil skim stones every time we are near water: either down at the river or in the big estate lake, which is about twenty minutes from our home. But today I have the greatest skimming stones you can ever imagine: slate. Millions of pieces of flat, grey slate. Normally it takes you a few minutes to gather enough smooth stones for a good skim, but here, wow, you are standing on a pile of them every time you take a step.

All the boys have been skimming, even some of the girls had a go, but they were rubbish. Everyone has drifted off now, just over the small hill of slate to start their packed lunches. I can just about hear their chattering. So I have this moment, this brief moment before I join them, when I am all alone, by this completely flat, turquoise oasis, skimming slate that skims and skims and skims, until it finally runs out of steam and disappears into the icy depths. The sky is blue, the sun is shining and twinkling off the water. Although it is cool, I am warm because I've been skimming for so long, my blue Parka coat is next to me on the ground. Just one more. OK, just one more. Alright, one more. I'll never be in a more beautiful place, surely. Not a care. Never a care. I can't stop smiling.

Back at the farm, it's late afternoon, and we have been told to have a 'quiet hour' by Mr Walker. But all the boys are lying on our bunks laughing and joking. We had been talking about how brilliant this school trip has been and comparing it to the boring trips to museums.

Stephen Roberts has just told us a hilarious story of when his mum and dad took him and his sister to a museum in London, the one with all the dinosaurs in. He had said that his sister was much younger than him and still in a pushchair, and she was asleep. His mum and dad were sat on a bench and Stephen was wheeling his sleeping sister around, close by. It was then that he spotted the enormous, life size model of a T-Rex's head, raised off the floor by about four feet; just about the right height to wheel a small pushchair under. Checking that his mum and dad weren't watching too closely, Stephen positioned their dosing daughter directly under the gapping mouth of the Tyrannosaurus. When Stephen was happy with the location of the buggy, he walked behind it, lent forward and clapped once, but loudly, in his sister's ear. He said the scream she gave out when she woke up, inches from the rows of needle sharp teeth, could be heard in the canteen, two floors down. Apparently, he got a bollocking similar to the level that I got when I smashed the kitchen window playing cricket with Neil. Severe, but not too severe, because, Stephen said, he could tell that his dad thought it was pretty funny as well.

The next day, the last day of the trip, we find ourselves on a windswept, deserted, pebble beach, full of little coves, caves and surrounded by high cliffs. Us boys are building a dam in a small stream that is running into the sea. We've pretty much blocked it up completely, so that the clear, fresh water of the stream is breaking its banks and finding alternative routes down to the sea.

Bored with that, we play chicken where the waves are breaking on the shore. Mr Walker has already told us to be careful, but someone's going to get wet feet for sure. The girls have clipboards with paper attached that has nature stuff on, and they are merrily ticking off what they've seen. "Oh look, a bird." "Oh look, some seaweed." "Oh look, the sea!" the girls keenly squeal.

We are walking back across the beach towards the bus. Brian Perkins is stumbling over the pebbles in his socks. He is wearing his shoes on his hands, like gloves and they are dripping wet. Just before we pass our dam (that has already been breached), I notice something weird between two large stones. I stop and kick the stones away as the other boys continue on. It's a seahorse. It's lovely, with its pointed snout and horsey like face. It is very dead though, so I pick it up. Christ, it's big, really big. I run after the other boys with the creature from the deep held tightly between my thumb and first finger. I catch up with them and waggle it around in front of their faces, so that they all hunch their shoulders and squirm a little, trying to avoid contact with it.

Back on the bus I show it to Mr Walker and Mrs Webster.

"Wow, that is big," they say, and Mrs Webster tears off a piece of newspaper she finds in the footwell of the passenger seat on the bus, and wraps the animal up and says that she will put it in the glove compartment. I think this is just as much to ensure that the boys don't annoy the girls with it on the trip back to the farm, as much as it is to keep it safe.

It's the last evening at the farm and the teachers and the girls have organised some games for everyone. The girls make the boys go outside the sitting room and call us in one by one. Every time a boy goes in, the door is shut behind them so the rest of us can't see. There is some talking, that we can't make out, ears pressed up against the large wooden door, followed by lots of girly laughter. I am fifth to go in. Just Tom and Kevin Straka after me. As I go in, I am presented with two queens (well Jessica Wakeman and Helen Walker – Mr Walker's daughter), complete with robes and crowns. They are sitting either end of what looks like a bench, covered in a duvet, with a space in the middle.

"Welcome, my King," Queens Jessica and Helen say in unison, "Pray, sit down with us a while, you must be weary." I look around for any clues from the four boys who have already been laughed at, but they are tight lipped. I am ushered to the bench, where another member of the royal court, Lisa Davies, puts a yellow, cardboard crown on my head.

"Do sit," she says. As I take my place on my 'throne,' the two queens immediately stand up, and, hilariously(?!), I fall through the empty space that awaits me under the duvet. The little monkeys. It's quite a good gag actually, even though most of the boys are reluctant to admit it.

Finally, and just before bed, we have a game called charades, or something. You get given the name of someone on a bit of paper and you have to act out who it is, without talking, for the other people in your team to guess. This is mildly amusing. Mrs Webster hands me her bit of paper when it is my turn. 'Mick Jagger,' it says on it. Never heard of him.

We are nearly home, the journey back has taken much longer than coming. We are all tired and moany and Lisa Davies, the courtier from last night, has just puked light brown vom' into a plastic bag. Apart from this, the trip has been brilliant. Mum's at the school to meet me. Life is ace. Double ace, actually, because it's bonfire night in a couple of weeks!

Back in school the following week, I am sat in Mr Walker's office. The school secretary (Mr Walker's wife) has just made a telephone call to the Natural History Museum in London. She hands the receiver to me, nodding excitedly. I am a bit nervous.

"Hello." I say, "Is that Professor Atkinson, at the Natural History Museum, in London?"

"Yes, it is." Comes the reply (he sounds a bit like Mr Hello from The Passage – the one without a telly).

"Oh, hello," I continue, "I've been told to talk to you because I have found a record breaking size seahorse on a beach in Wales last week on a school trip and…"

"OK, fabulous," says the Professor. I could sense the raising excitement in his voice as he cuts me off. "Can you tell me how big it is, have you measured it in centimetres?

"Yes, I have" I announce proudly, picking up the creature

and looking at it for the hundredth time. "It is thirty-one centimetres long."

"Goodness me!" Says the Professor. I assume he is standing up now, in his dusty old office, looking through the phone book for the telephone number of Roy Castle or Norris McSquirer from BBC's Record Breakers.

"Can you just tell me, young man, is the body of the seahorse at ninety degrees to the head?" I know what ninety degrees means and I confirm to him, confidently, that it is not. "No, I say, the seahorse's body comes straight out from the seahorse's head."

There is a pause on the line. Then finally Professor Atkinson says, "Unfortunately, what you have found," in what I think is a slightly irritated way, "is a pipefish, not a seahorse. Perhaps it would have been better if one of your teachers had checked in a book before calling the Natural History Museum. Goodbye." The line goes dead and I hand the receiver back to Mrs Walker and she places it gently on the large cream phone.

"Well?" she says eagerly.

"Pipefish, apparently," I say, only mildly disappointed.

"Oh well." says Mrs Walker. "We'll keep it in the cabinet in the corridor, along with the stuffed ferrets and stoats. Does it smell?"

"Only a bit," I reply and I skip out into the playground.

Chapter 18

Louise and I had met when we were both eighteen, at Nottingham Polytechnic in 1987. We were on the same course, a BTEC Higher National Diploma in Business Studies. Dull, I know, but it was pretty much my only avenue after some spectacularly poor 'A' level results. Still, I had always wanted to go to University (well Poly', as it turned out). Neil, my brother, was in his last year at Liverpool Polytechnic, and having visited him there a couple of times and having a great laugh, I knew it was time to leave Lambe, mum and dad, and start the next chapter of my life.

I hadn't really noticed Louise on the course and it was her who approached me, towards the end of the first term around Christmas. She edged up to me in the crowded student union bar, both pissed, and that was it really. We stayed together throughout college and moved to London together to study a one year postgraduate course in personnel management (I know, dull again, but hey, it pays the bills now).

We lived together for the first time in Hendon High Street in a pokey, but quite cool, attic room in a small house, next door to the Prince of Ceylon Indian Restaurant. It was freezing cold, however, so we moved to a boring one-bed, in a purpose built block of flats, about a twenty minute walk to the college. Living together was great at first, but we were both a bit restless and when we started our first jobs in London, we decided to stay together but live in different houses: Louise in Finchley, me in Muswell Hill – living with my brother, Neil and my friend Jack. The same Jack who I stay with in London now for two nights a week.

Louise and I probably should have split up at that point. But we kept it going, and when my brother moved to Blackheath in South London and Jack went on his way, I moved into Louise's flat. We've lived together ever since. In 1996, nearly ten years after we had first met, we bought our first home. A two bedroomed flat in Finchley and on the day we moved in, I got a phone call from Louise's work (she worked as a sales assistant for a clothes shop in Covent Garden), saying that she had slipped over in the shop and had broken her arm really badly, and was in a central London hospital.

Her arm break was pretty bad and she needed morphine for the pain and a night in hospital. I had to move in on my own and so it wasn't the best start to our lives as home owners. A year later our close friends got married after a similar time together and it was the prompt I seemed to need to propose to Louise. We married in 1997 but Louise continued to have serious bouts of depression that she'd had since college, when I look back on it. We were both concerned about having children at first because of the Lithium tablets that Louise was on. However, after reassurances from a couple of doctors, we decided to go for it and Alex came along in 1999 and Emma two years later.

As I walked back down to the hospital on this bright and sunny Wednesday morning, following my night at Clic house, I realised that my life had just sort of fallen into place. I hadn't steered it too much. Louise and I had had some great times. College was fun, we'd had great holidays; New York in 1995 was brilliant, paid for with a bonus she had got from work. Kos in 1998, when we had finally decided to have kids, was a relaxing paradise. We had good friends and a good social life. But was I deeply in love with her? I wasn't sure I ever had been, not really.

I felt sad for myself and for my thoughts about Louise. But it was time to re-energise. To look after my wife and my family. I'd had a good night's sleep at Clic house and I felt fresher than I had for days.

My new found optimism was rewarded when I got onto ward thirty-four. A nurse, that I was familiar with but I couldn't remember her name, saw me come through the doors and met me with a smile and ushered me away from the main bedded ward and down the corridor, where the four, precious, exclusive side rooms are. We got to the last door but one on the left and as I looked through the window I could see Emma and Louise fast asleep, together, peacefully on the bed.

"I won't disturb them." I whispered to the nurse, unnecessarily because the door was shut and pretty thick.

"I need to go in anyway and take some blood in a sec', so you may as well go in," the nurse said, and pointed to the hand sanitiser dispensing unit on the wall. I released a large dollop into my hands and rubbed them together. I pushed the door open with my foot and sat in the chair by the bed, trying not to wake them (I thought I would leave that to the nurse when she came back), but Louise woke up anyway, and after a few stretches, I gave her and Emma a kiss.

"Well, this is nice," I say, cheerily, looking around our new, spacious (though slightly clinical) one bedroomed, Bristol apartment. Louise smiled and we hugged.

Professor Elmwood arrived with his gang at about ten o'clock. It took about five minutes from the time I saw them outside the room, to the last doctor coming in and closing the door. It had taken this long because each of them had to put on a white plastic apron and gloves. Professor Elmwood headed straight for Emma's tummy.

"OK," he said, we held our breath... "Some better news"... and relax. "Well, two bits of news actually," he continued. "First, the x-ray of Emma's tummy doesn't show any abnormalities, just large pockets of air, that are not necessarily unusual. I will expect her tummy to probably go down a little bit over the next few days, so we will keep an eye on that. Now, secondly and more importantly, we have the results of Emma's blood test from last night. What we are looking for in this blood test is the eradication of the leukaemic cells. You may remember that I told you, when you first arrived, that it is important that we see that the chemotherapy does this in a very short space of time. I'm pleased to say that this has happened in Emma's case."

I laugh out loud. I don't mean to but it is such a relief. We were due some good news and we got it. The Prof. could see I was really happy and acknowledged me with a nod and a smile.

Professor Elmwood continued, "It is a good sign, quick remission is important, but as I said before, we have to do everything we can to ensure it stays away, and this is the hard part." I'll take it, I'll take it, so please don't say anything shit now to ruin it, I think to myself. And he doesn't. I get the feeling he could, but I think he senses he should leave it at that for now.

"I'll see you tomorrow," he says, tearing his apron off. The other doctors follow suit and one by one they file out of the door, leaving the three of us to our peaceful little sanctuary of a room, with a tiny, tiny, weeny bit of good news to hang on to.

I decide to do a bit of a tour of our new living quarters. We have our own bathroom and, and well that's about it. We do have a telly on the wall and a window that looks out over the front of the hospital. I can see the lollipop statue outside, the main road and a view over the city to the south.

I'm feeling OK. I will be staying here tonight, and the big chair that folds out into a bed for parents to sleep on, looks infinitely more comfy than the ones on the ward.

I wonder which new cancer victim will be heading for Emma's vacated bed on the ward, bed one. It might be a kid who hasn't been diagnosed yet. A kid who doesn't know why they're feeling so poorly. A kid, whose parents are concerned about why their little one hasn't recovered from that cold. Scary thoughts, and we had been there only five days ago.

Chapter 19

Bonfire night

I wake up earlier than I normally would on a Sunday. The reason is, tonight, it is bonfire night. Still plenty of time then for us to make this year's village bonfire even bigger than it was last year. And last year it was massive. The village bonfire is always bang in the middle of The Green, which is a patch of grass in the centre of the village, that is a triangle shape and about the size of... well, a village green. The Green is surrounded by three quiet roads and at the point where two of these roads meet, is our house.

The bonfire is about a twenty second walk from my front door. The fire is so big it leaves a pile of embers that smoulder away for a week, meaning small boys can light sticks in the hot ashes for days after. The burnt ring, made by the fire, leaves a large scar on The Green, and the grass only just starts to grow back before the next load of wood is piled on top of it the following year.

The build-up to a Lambe bonfire night is, like Halloween, an event in itself. First, there is the fund raising for the fireworks. The more money raised, the bigger and better the display. This year has been a bumper year: cake stalls, fancy dress parties, tombolas, have all contributed to the firework pot, organised by Mr Hutchens, the man who runs the youth club. There is a rumour that old Hutchens has got enough money for two Land Mines. Now Land Mines are really expensive at five pounds each (I know this because I've seen them in Woolworths in Witney). They are about as big as my leg and make a noise so loud that you can't hear anything after they go off. I reckon it is what they used to blow up the German trenches at the end of World War I (we just did a project on the war with Mr Walker in school. I love those old, funny looking tanks...). Anyway, Mr Hutchens could only afford one last year, so a double Land Mine this year will be ace. Windows will be shattered, but hopefully not at my house.

Whilst the money is being raised, the boys set about building the bonfire. This is sort of under the supervision of Mr Hutchins, but not really. He can't control the older lads from secondary school, who drag enormous amounts of combustible material from all four corners of the village, and pile it up, up, up, until you need a huge ladder and a head for heights just to stick poor old Guy Fawkes on the top of it.

In the build-up to 'the 5th,' on the Friday before, we are usually privileged to be entertained by some of the naughtier, older boys in Tom Tate's brother's year. They put on a little show all of their own. This year Mark Skelly was the star. It was about six thirty in the evening and dark (there are no street lights in Lambe), when Mark Skelly dragged a mattress from off the side of the bonny (yes, really, a mattress, we put anything we can on it). He poured petrol onto the mattress from a plastic squash bottle.

Mark Skelly is the only fifteen year old in the village who has two, proper, motorised go-karts (his mum and dad are loaded), and therefore he has easy access to flammable liquids. Whilst he is struggling to locate his lighter in his leather look, black plastic jacket, some of his mates build little ramps either side of the mattress. Watching this build-up are about ten or twelve lads, of which me and Tom are probably the youngest. No adults are present, although carefully located lookouts will warn everyone if some grown-ups do decide to come out and interfere.

It hasn't been raining, so the mattress is nice and dry and it goes up with a good old whoosh. Everyone takes a step back. Backing up his blue Chopper to get a decent run up, Mark Skelly looks like Evel Knievel (or Eddie Kidd, Evel's UK rival).

Mark's first attempt to jump the length of flaming mattress comes to a front wheeled, skidding stop at the base of the take off ramp. The wheel digs into the soft grass of The Green, but he controls it well. Not enough speed, I guess, to get him to safety. So 'Skelly' turns and heads back to his mark, the tension mounting, nervous spectators (knowing full well that this is all very wrong) roar him on.

It's a quality jump. Flames licking at his white Adidas trainers and frayed bell bottoms, he makes it across with room to spare. Big cheers all around, then the bigger boys flick the mattress over and the flames are extinguished immediately. In an instant it is pitch black again, and as quickly as the crowd appeared, it disappears into the night. Me and Tom head back to my house for hot chocolate and a little lie to mum about what we've been doing for the past half an hour.

It has been such an exciting past few days in the build-up to bonfire night. Halloween this year was again a scream, but it was nothing compared to meeting Han Solo. Yep, for real, Han.

If you turn left out of my house, in about fifteen minutes you get to Witney. If you turn right, in about the same time you end up in Woodstock. A pretty little town, Woodstock houses the gates of Blenheim Palace, the place where Winston Churchill was born. But on this cold Wednesday night in November 1978, Woodstock has been turned into Nazi headquarters. Draped all over the townhall and the buildings that surround the square are enormous, black, red and white Swastika flags. Winston would be turning in his grave. The town is set up as a scene for a new Hollywood film called Hanover Street (or Leg Over Street as me and Tom are calling it), in which Han Solo is playing the lead role. Nothing like this has ever happened to anyone living around here.

Me, mum, Neil, Tom, Brian Perkins (from my class) and Stephen 'Welly' Wilkins (Neil's friend), are standing behind a metal barrier along with dozens of other people. It's cold, and my mum's getting bored because we have been here for an hour and a half and nothing has happened; except a few Nazi's wandering about with modern day coats on, with what, I guess, must be scripts in their hands. Everyone is waiting for Han. Of course, we all saw Star Wars last year at the ABC cinema in Oxford. Everyone loved it, except my mum, who fell asleep.

At last, a man with a megaphone tells everyone to be quiet, and following a long pause, someone else shouts, "ACTION!"

Out of the corner of the square, to our right, a group of four or five men in grey German uniforms, carrying machine-guns, run towards the townhall entrance, right in front of us. As the soldiers skip up the steps to the hall (a huge Nazi flag fluttering above them), one of the men trips, drops his gun and it flies, noisily, across the cobble stoned courtyard.

"CUT!" The same voice shouts. I realise I've been holding my breath, and breathe deeply through puffed cheeks. I look around and notice Neil and Tom are doing the same thing. Even mum looks like the hour and a half wait has finally been worth it. The soldier that had fallen, picks himself up, and soon the actors are surrounded by people with white plastic cups in their hands. Was it Han that fell? Tom doesn't think so and points to the soldier at the far left of the group. It was him. Han Solo. Wow.

We hang around for a further half an hour, as there are rumours in the crowd that the captain of the Millennium Falcon would be signing autographs. But it doesn't happen and so the crowd slowly slips away and we did too.

When we got home it was quite late but mum let us have a snack before bed. I decided to have some of my favourite cereal, Golden Nuggets. On the back of the packet is a scene from Star Wars. It's the one where Luke and Leia are on a Star Destroyer (or is it the Death Star?) and are being chased by stormtroopers; they get stuck and have to swing across a gap to safety. Me and Neil have already put all the transfer stickers onto the scene: Luke, Leia, the stormtroopers and all their laser fire. Unfortunately, Han isn't in this scene, but who cares, we've seen him in real life.

***

Back to Sunday morning, the 5th November. I have a stretch and do a little 'bicycle kick' movement in bed with my legs, to warm myself up. I pull back my yellow duvet that has clouds on it and a farm, and shiver a little as I draw the curtains to see if the bonfire has got any bigger overnight.

My bedroom window looks out over The Green, and you can just about see the bonny through the leafless branches of the copper beech tree that grows next to our drive. Each of the twelve small panes that make up my bedroom window are covered in condensation, so I use the sleeve of my (slightly too small) Mr Benn pyjama top to clear one of the panes. As I peer through the half clear glass, I can see that it is quite a misty morning and the view to The Green is obscured. But something isn't right. I rub the glass hard with my now wet sleeve and jump onto the bed to get a closer look out of the window. Oh my God, something is terribly wrong.

Through the mist I can see that the biggest and best bonfire ever created by Lambe's finest, has gone! The smoke from the remains mixes with the fog and eerily covers the handful of people who have started to gather around the ambers that are faintly glowing. I check my Casio digi' watch; it's eight thirty-seven AM.

***

It's six forty-five in the evening on the same day, the 5th November 1978. Mr Hutchens is about to start the firework display. He has a glowing taper in his hand and I have a sparkler in mine, writing my name with it and stuff like that. Behind me, is a bonfire that has just been lit and is beginning to take hold. Guy Fawkes sits on the top, twenty feet in the air! This new bonfire, built from scratch this morning, this phoenix of a bonny, is half as big again as the one that was prematurely and criminally burnt to the ground last night. How can this possibly be? Because this is my village, and anything is possible!

Armies of children of all ages, with their parents and grandparents, began to mass on The Green by about nine o'clock in the morning. By ten o'clock dozens of five feet square pallets had appeared from somewhere. Mums and dads were dragging garden waste, wood and cardboard from all parts of the village. Ford Cortinas and Vauxhall Vivas arrived with burnable materials strapped to their roofs; more mattresses protruding from their open boots.

By two thirty in the afternoon the bonfire was nearly back to its original size. Me, Tom, Neil, 'Welly', Jim Tate and a couple of other older boys are working together, in the rain, up in the woods beyond the bus shelter on Woodstock Street. We are surrounded by other teams of boys doing exactly the same thing. Cutting down trees, yes, trees. Not oaks or beech or massive stuff, but pretty big trees all the same. Someone's got a little radio with them, Blondie's

'Heart of Glass' crackles out in the drizzle.

Once we have got through the trees with our dad's saws, they are dragged behind bikes, attached with rope and pulled down the hill and onto The Green; where men chuck them onto the ever increasing mound. If cars come the other way, and potentially block or slow down our logging process, kids and grown-ups alike, politely tell them to park on the verges and let the Choppers and Grifters through. Some drivers of the cars, you can tell, cannot believe their eyes, as boys with long, wet hair, in flared cords and polo neck jumpers, cycle passed them with twenty feet trees, branches and brown leaves dragging behind them. By five o'clock it was dark but still the mountain grew higher.

When it was time for this miracle to be lit, it had stopped raining and there were hundreds of people on The Green. Twice as many as usual and there are normally loads. Lambe only has a few hundred residents, so I guess most of them were here. There is never any rope around the bonny to stop you getting too close; as far as I know, no one has ever been burnt alive since I've lived here, or any time before. I guess, quite rightly, they don't expect people to just jump into the flames. This means we get a great view of the fire as it goes up; the immediate heat taking your breath away, as you take your coat hood down and unzip your Parka. Everyone is lighting sparklers in the flames.

There is no great speech by someone mildly important on the parish council, about how great we all are to build this replacement bonfire in eight hours etc etc. Everyone just accepts that it needed to be done. No meetings, no organisation, just friendly village people getting on with it and doing what was right.

After the second Land Mine goes off, I can see Tom is mouthing something to me. I can't hear what he's saying yet because I am still partially deafened by the detonation of the high explosives. "What?" I shout.

"You know who they reckon burnt our bonfire down?" Tom repeats, moving closer.

"Who's that?" I reply.

"Well, the police caught them setting fire to the one in Kenbury, as well. They were definitely from Stonesford and one of them, we reckon, was the older brother of that boy who knocked my brother's tooth out with that catapult on the bridge."

"Yeah, I bet it was." I say. We turn, look up and smile as the massive orange flames melt the football head of Guy Fawkes.

Chapter 20

The new occupant of bed one, our old bed, is a boy called Allister. He came in last night and is quite a bit older than Emma. He doesn't seem too unwell, but his parents look as shell shocked as we did when we first came in. It is not long before Allister has a bandage around his hand, a cannula sticking out of it and he's lassoed to a machine.

I slept in the side room with Emma last night for the first time and had a reasonable night's sleep. The nurses kept coming in and out all night, doing their checks and taking blood, but it is so much better than being on the ward. Emma was still asleep at nine o'clock, so I went to get a coffee. As I pass the entrance to the main ward, I can see from their grim, tired faces, that poor Allister and his mother had not had the best night's sleep in their new home.

When I got back to the side room with my coffee (I'm sick of the stuff already), I thought I would try out the telly. I hadn't really watched any programmes since this all began a few days ago; I'd just had to listen to them via the other noisy sets on the ward. Anyway, Emma and I had our own TV now and I intended to play it as loud as possible - I won't of course, that would be moronic. I put BBC news on.

Not much happening in the world, just another Gulf War about to take place! "Weapons of Mass Destruction," is the new phrase constantly blurting out of every politician and newsreader. As we are fighting our own little battle three-thousand miles away, I decide to switch over to Channel 5 and watch Spot the Dog, even though Emma is still asleep.

I'm still watching children's telly when Louise arrives at about ten o'clock, followed by Professor Elmwood and his troops. We all exchange pleasantries and then the lanky Professor sits on the edge of the bed. Here we go.

He opens with, "We need to carry out a few more tests on Emma, they are routine, but all very important. The first is a chromosome test, it's actually called the 'Philadelphia' test and we need to send that sample away to be analysed, so it might be a few weeks before we get it back."

My head is full of questions, like, "Why can't they analyse the test at this hospital? "How many weeks are we talking about here?" and, "Why is a chromosome test named after a Tom Hanks film?" I keep my thoughts to myself.

The Professor continues, "The chromosome sample is analysed for some genetic information, which can be important in determining the potential for future relapse in A.L.L. sufferers. The other important tests are the bone marrow tests, I think I mentioned these before. We have to take samples when Emma is under general anaesthetic, so we will do this when she is in theatre having her lumber puncture injections. You'll remember, this is when we need to get the chemo' into her spinal column."

"Oh yeah, I hadn't forgot that," I remind myself with a grimace.

"We will need to do a few of these bone marrow checks and each are important to understand whether the leukaemic cells are being reproduced or not. Do you have any questions about any of what I've said?" The Professor concludes. We shake our heads.

Chapter 21

Dad and mum

My dad is an agent: a special agent? A secret agent? Neither, he's a travel agent, but he is special to me. He is a manager for Thomas Cook. He looks a little bit like Al Pacino, but he is taller and he is no gangster. He's not from the south of Italy, like Michael Corleone, but from the north; the smart bit, Genoa.

The history of his family (well, I guess it is my family as well) is fascinating, absolutely fascinating. He came to England when he was about eighteen years old in 1952. His father was a Genoese Count, his grandfather was a Count, his great grandfather was a Count, and his great, great grandfather was a Count. You get the picture. That makes my dad a Count, and yes, I guess that makes me and my brother little Counts as well.

We can trace the Italian line of our family history back to the 8th Century AD. Amazing hey! I know this because we have an enormous family tree, in a frame, which has lots of little circles on it with Italian names written in them, with their dates of births and deaths. The family tree is on very old yellowy/brown paper and in the corner a little bit of it has been burnt.

You can't read all the names in the little circles because they are a bit faded and written in swirly, whirly ink. I spend hours on the stairs staring up at this unusual thing hanging on our wall, something that I've never seen in any of my friends' houses.

I don't fully understand why we are not living in a castle, but dad said something about his parents losing most of their possessions during the Second World War. He would know, he was in Italy with his parents and his sister in 1943, when the Italians changed sides in the war. My dad told me and Neil the whole story a couple of weeks ago, just before he went on a business trip to Washington DC in America. It was over Sunday lunch, spaghetti alle vongole, which my dad had just cooked. Me and Neil sat open mouthed, letting our pasta go cold as he told his real life story.

Apparently, his family had thirty minutes notice to escape from the Germans when the Italians sided with the British. Although my grandfather was a Count, in 1943 he worked as the vice consul, or something, for the Italian embassy, just over the north eastern Italian border, in Yugoslavia. Now, my dad's mother was English (well Scottish actually), which made things very complicated and very dangerous. She was from a rich family from Aberdeenshire and had fallen for the Italian Count when on holiday on the Italian Rivera in the 1920's.

Because my grandfather worked for the embassy, he was fortunate that he got news quite early that the Italians were about to dump their evil Nazi partners and fight for the allies. However, this meant that the Germans would soon be slaughtering Italian troops and civilians because they still occupied most of Italy.

My grandfather left work in his black embassy car and drove at speed back to the family villa. He gathered up a tiny amount of possessions: his wife, my dad and his sister and their dog, a blue tongued chow called Pong. The nanny or 'schwester' as she was known, also piled into the back of the car. She was German (to add to this complicated situation), and my grandfather knew that she would not survive if she was caught by the Nazi's, because she worked for a British/Italian family. Being a German would not have saved her. My dad was ten years old, my age now. His sister was eight.

First stop was to an eccentric woman's house down the street, who looked after numerous stray dogs. My grandfather leapt out of the black saloon, gently ushered the dog off the back seat, to the sounds of his daughter's (my Auntie's) cries and led the dog down the rhododendron lined path of the large house, where he met the strangely dressed woman in her sixties. She took Pong's lead and, reluctantly, the large handful of lire that my grandfather insisted on giving her.

Trying not to show his emotions at leaving his beloved chow, my grandfather walked quickly (though not running), elegantly, proudly, back to his car; four frightened faces staring at him through the windows.

Next stop, was the docks. My dad can't remember exactly where, but it was, he said, at the northern tip of the Adriatic Sea that runs all the way down the eastern side of Italy. The forty-five minute car journey to the port (after dropping off the dog), was fraught with danger. Two check points were successfully negotiated, nervously, but fortunately my grandfather's diplomatic paperwork still held some weight (as did the wedge of money he used to slip his family through the guarded security gates).

Once at the docks, the car was abandoned by its five occupants (a middle ranking German officer, no doubt, acquired the car for himself in the days that followed).

My grandfather heaved the large, leather suitcase out of the trunk, charmed a dock official, and the five refugees headed quickly towards an enormous tanker, docked at the far end of the quay. The tanker was empty of its cargo, my dad realising this much later on because it was so high out of the water. My Grandfather led his family and their nanny up the incredibly steep gangplank, normally reserved for rough, Italian sailors. My dad said he had to help his mother up the last part of the plank. She was dressed in high heels, an expensive skirt and fur coat. Tucked, tightly under her right arm, was her jewellery box.

After two days at sea, the tanker, heading south for the port of Bari, caught up with a hospital ship, clearly labelled with a large red cross on its deck. My dad's ship was about eight-hundred metres behind the hospital ship when the Stuka fighter bomber came out of the blue skies above the Adriatic.

My dad and his sister were stood at the front of the ship with a handful of other lucky escapees (who could afford to pay the mercenary skipper of the tanker), as they watched the German plane drop three bombs onto the hospital ship. Dad said that everyone around him instinctively ducked when two of the bombs landed dead centre on the hapless boat. The third bomb exploded in the water, sending up a huge plume of spray into the air. The screams from the women passengers around my father were nothing compared to the panic that followed, when the Stuka bomber was seen again behind my dad's ship, swooping down, engines roaring, about to attack them.

My grandparents, by this time, had grabbed their children and headed to another part of the ship; although my dad remembers that nowhere looked safe. Their nanny, cowered with others around the main funnel: eyes closed, arms folded around her chest, cigarette between her tightly pursed lips.

Dad says, that he remembers looking up at the plane as it flew directly over the ship and seeing the menacing black crosses on the distinctive, angular wings; but no bombs came. Later, dad could only think (or he may have been told), that the cowardly pilot of the Stuka, had dropped the last of his deadly payload onto the unfortunate hospital ship and luckily, had no more bombs to destroy my dad and his family with. If he had, I guess, we wouldn't be sat around our kitchen table, in the peaceful Cotswolds, fork and spoon in hand, mouths gaping.

My dad's ship picked up one (just one!) survivor in the water from the boat that had sunk amazingly quickly, down to the bottom of the Adriatic Sea. The survivor was unconscious when he was somehow hauled up the side of the oil tanker. He had a large, dirty, white bandage around his chest and back that was splattered with blood, from what looked like bullet wounds. Presumably, these injuries were the reason why he had been on the hospital ship in the first place.

Dad said that he didn't remember much more about the sea journey until they arrived at Bari a few days later; just a few fights between drunken sailors. He was told, many years later by his father, that they were extremely lucky not to have been sunk by one of the many sea mines that littered that narrow seaway that runs down to the, now peaceful, Mediterranean, where we have been on a few family summer holidays.

The British naval destroyers that now guarded the docks at Bari in 1943, only offered short lived relief and safety to the refugees fleeing the north of their war torn country. One night, soon after they had got off their ship, the docks at Bari were bombed by German planes, trying to take back this strategic seaport. My dad and his family were sheltering in a large house a few hundred metres away, sat on mattresses and chairs, the place full of cigarette smoke. He remembers enormous explosions, the lights going out and a door of the room being blown in, striking a woman on the head. She was badly injured, her head covered in blood, but everyone else was alright, apart from the shock.

I took a mouthful of spaghetti wrapped around my fork, and thought about how easy my ten year old life was; playing army down the river with plastic guns and generally titting about, completely carefree. At the same age my dad had been in a proper war zone.

Years later, my grandfather told my dad that when they escaped the Germans on that fateful day in 1943, he had taken his Beretta pistol from the drawer in his office and put it into his suit jacket pocket. In the chamber of the gun, were just three bullets. My grandfather later confessed to his son, that if it had ever come to it, he would have shot my dad, his sister and his own wife, rather than leave them to the mercy of the Nazis. Wow.

My dad's family, finally ended up in Sicily, where they stayed for the next year and a half, or so, until the war was over. He remembers some of the local 'scugnizzo' peasant boys, throwing stones at him, but he fought back, he always fought back. They didn't do it again. On another day he saw these same street kids catch and slit the throat of a wild goat. He remembers them, playfully drumming on the dead animal's belly. Unfortunately, he wasn't unused to seeing such cruelties to animals.

A couple of years earlier, back in the north of Italy in the first year of the war, he remembered that a troop of mounted German soldiers came clattering down the cobbled street near to their villa. Lying in the road were dozens of stray cats, warming themselves in the early morning spring sun. If he hadn't have pressed himself against the wall, my dad would have been flattened by the horses, galloping down the street, pompously ridden by their German, uniformed cavalrymen.

Whilst my dad survived the hooves, the same could not be said for all of the cats, which now lay dead and dying, flattened against the cobbles. He choked up a bit when he told us that. Then he quickly moved on when my mum gave him a stare (it was lunchtime remember). However, this frightful scene clearly stuck with him.

On another day, dad had told us the fate of their dog, Pong. His father, my grandfather, had told my dad what happened to their dog, many years later, when my dad was much older. Apparently, twenty-four hours after my grandfather had dropped their beloved dog off at the eccentric woman's house, a group of German soldiers marched down the rhododendron lined path and knocked on her door. It had now been confirmed that the Italians were definitely changing sides and the German revenge against Italians was swift and ruthless. Apparently, after inviting themselves into the woman's home, the soldiers pushed her out of the way and went to the numerous kennels out the back of the large house. There, a captain instructed one of the soldiers to shoot all the dogs, dozens of them. Pong was amongst those who were machine-gunned. Cruelly, they did not shoot the kind woman, but left her to grieve on her knees amongst the dead and half dead animals.

Once the war was over, my dad's family moved back to the north of Italy for a few months, living with friends in elegant Milan; the after effects of the war still present amongst the city and its people. My dad remembers the huge cathedral there, and playing in the dusty park around the back of a castle. But he wasn't there for long. His father, my grandfather, took up his job with the Italian embassy again, and was posted to India. Their nanny was released from their service and went to Switzerland to work. Dad remembers travelling first to the Middle East and waiting somewhere (he couldn't remember where), for a boat to take them, first class, to India.

When they were waiting the few weeks for the boat to arrive, dad remembered, down by the port, a large number of poor, filthy looking people piling off a large passenger ship. He could just make out, beneath the grime, that their ragged clothes had blue and white stripes on them. Later, he would realise that these men, women and children were the survivors of the recently liberated German concentration camps, making their way, still in their dirty uniforms, to their new home. We had talked about the Jews during our war project in school last term, it was very sad.

Once my dad, his sister, mother and father arrived in India, he was sent to boarding school in one part of this vast, strange country. His sister, my aunty, was sent somewhere else. His father went about his embassy business (not sure what that was, but dad says it involved going to parties with lots of important people). His mother, on the other hand, wrote a couple of novels: one about a Russian Princess, the other a romantic thriller.

My dad only saw his mother and father during the holidays and, after a year or so, they all moved over the border to the newly formed Pakistan; where he went to a school in a place called Panchgani. I remember this, because dad said that the lead singer of Queen, Freddie Mercury, went to the very same school (though not at the same time as my dad). Bohemian Rhapsody is one of my favourite songs. It's a sort of 'rock opera,' they say. My dad doesn't like it, he prefers real opera. Anyway, at school, he said he remembers eating chapatis for breakfast and learning how to box; which came in handy if he ever got picked on, which wasn't often after the first time.

My dad was about fifteen years old when his father retired, and whilst my grandmother and grandfather moved back to northern Italy, to the Riviera in San Remo, my dad and his sister were sent to boarding schools in England. My dad was packed off to Gloucestershire, his sister to London.

Dad spent a couple of years at this posh school, sometimes going back to Italy in the holidays to see his parents, sometimes not. He rarely saw his sister. He had to do army national service after school, he didn't really enjoy it, but he did another year voluntarily because he didn't know what job to do. He wished he hadn't when his regiment nearly got called up to fight in Korea. But he got lucky and they sent some other poor sods instead.

He met my mum in London. He had started working as an 'agent' with Thomas Cook, and she was at teacher training college in South London. They met at a party in Piccadilly, and took a tube and then a midnight walk towards Buckingham Palace. It was 1958; she was nineteen and he was twenty-four. He said she was beautiful. She is as well; the Countess, my mum.

I never met my dad's father, my grandfather, he died many years before I was born. My dad said it was of a broken heart. You see in 1965, my dad's sister died in an aeroplane crash at Heathrow airport. She was an air stewardess for B.E.A and was on a flight between Edinburgh and London, when her passenger plane crashed in the fog whilst attempting to land. Everyone on board was killed. It was at a time when stewardesses looked like film stars and were the envy of most women throughout the world. She was only twenty-nine, and her name was Fiamma. My dad told me, with tears in his eyes, that 'Fiamma,' in Italian, means: 'Consumed by flames.' It was a tragedy.

Apparently, my grandfather never recovered from the grief of losing his precious daughter. How terrible that must have been for him, as a father? I never met my aunty, Fiamma, but I reckon I would have liked her.

I did meet my dad's mother (my grandma, my nona) a few times, but she died about three years ago when I was seven. She was very old, but very elegant. She wore diamonds and jewels all the time when she used to stay with us, and sometimes a fur coat. I wonder if it was the same fur coat and jewels that she wore and carried up the gangplank of that oil tanker when they escaped the Nazis in 1943?

Chapter 22

It's two weeks since cancer has taken over our lives. Emma is getting worse and worse, not better and better. The doctors try to reassure us that it is the treatment that is making her so ill, but how can such a tiny thing be put through this? Her plight is made worse by the fact that she has picked up this Norwalk virus. Professor Elmwood has explained that the chemo' treatment is at fault for much of her pain, but they, the hospital, are responsible for the Norwalk infection she caught off the ward. I could tell he was slightly embarrassed by this, but I appreciated his honesty, and I trust him implicitly. You could say I trust him with my daughter's life, because I have to.

Emma is listless and moany, the steroids are making her agitated and hungry. But the chemo' apparently affects the taste buds, so when she tries to eat something, she invariably spits it out. Taste is so badly affected in fact, that it led to one of the nurses explaining that chocolate, for example, is often described (presumably by older patients than Emma) of tasting like shit, literally.

The chemo' and steroids are battering her immune system and she is starting to get temperatures regularly. She has observations every two hours. As soon as a temperature is registered from the ear thermometers, bloods are taken immediately, tested and antibiotics administered; either down her nose tube directly into her tummy, or down a line into her bloodstream through the cannula in her hand.

Sometimes the initial antibiotics don't work and her temperature goes dangerously off the scale. You can tell when the doctors come around that they are always concerned about the infections.

As parents, your initial reaction is to make sure that she doesn't come in contact with anyone with a cold because her immune system is so low. But we quickly recognise that it is the infections that she gets from her own body not working properly, that are so dangerous. Shingles is mentioned daily, but she hasn't got it yet.

The nights are long and uncomfortable, even in this relatively peaceful side room. I look forward to my alternate nights at Clic house, but then I worry when I'm there about what I'm missing on the ward. Emma really needs to have this Hickman line put into her chest so that they can administer her drugs more effectively. But because of the infections, they can't risk putting her under general anesthetic. Every positive thing they try to do, has a negative reaction. One step forward, two back.

So, this unpleasant routine drags on, day after day, night after night for all of us: mum, dad, Alex, Louise, her parents, me, and of course, Emma. We are all tied into this cruel event, our lives on hold, the humour sucked out of us. Laughter replaced by weeping. A different war in a desert rages on.

Chapter 23

Christmas

My mum is laughing at my dad. It's Christmas morning 1978 and we are opening our presents in our home, Catterpie Cottage. It is a small(ish) cottage, four bedrooms, cosy and quaint. When we first moved here seven years ago, when I was three and Neil was four or five, the cottage only had two bedrooms so me and Neil shared. Mum and dad made it bigger and now we've got our own bedrooms.

I think my mum and dad get on pretty well. They have rows sometimes and I sit on the top of the stairs to see what it is about. I normally can't hear properly, so I go off to bed. My mum is a school teacher; she actually works at my primary school. Luckily, she is not my teacher though, she teaches the little ones. Even though it is a small school, our paths don't cross too much; I don't bother her, which means she doesn't bother me. That's the rules.

When she first met my dad at that party in London and they walked around Buckingham Palace, she thought my dad was pretty cool, being an Italian Count and all. They got married in 1961 (the date is on a small black and white photograph in the living room) and they had my brother about five years later. I came along in 1968.

My mum's not from the same type of family as my dad. Her mum, my grandma, used to work in a factory and her dad, who I never met because he is dead, also worked in the same factory. They made brushes in Gloucestershire. My mum's mum, my grandma, is still alive. She is here with us for Christmas. She ties with my mum's friend, Delia, for being the nicest person in the world.

My mum and dad first lived together in London and then in Gloucestershire for a few years, but when my dad got a job in Oxford, we moved to this lovely village of Lambe.

So, it's Christmas and my mum is laughing at my dad because he has brought some presents back from his Washington DC business trip. He has wrapped them really badly and I mean really badly. However, as it turns out, the presents inside are not worthy of better packaging. What he has done, you see, is gather up as many free business gifts as he could possibly carry, from whatever travel agency conference he had been on, and then offered them up as presents to his sons. He is laughing now as Neil opens what looks like another money box with 'Thomas Cook' written on the side of it. We don't get that much pocket money and this is the third money box that we have opened this morning. After fighting our way into a dozen, tightly wrapped biros with 'Thomas Cook' written on them, dad gives in to our disappointed little faces and drags out our main presents from behind the tree.

Two skateboards, one each, obviously: helmets, knee and elbow pads. The skateboards are black with red wheels. 'Speed Boards' they are called and after some hugs and stuff, we are out in the drizzle, on the road outside the house, falling over for the next three hours until lunch.

Tom and a few other boys are outside the house as well, with their new boards. Tom and Neil are both pretty good straight away. Neil's friend 'Welly,' is absolutely brilliant.

But then 'Welly' is good on anything with wheels. He is always the fastest on any bike he is ever put on. He loves motor racing, as I do, and he has super powers when it comes to racing anything. No other boy, older or younger, has ever beaten 'Welly' in a bike race in the village.

The hill outside the house goes down to the park, but before you get there you pass the church on the right-hand side. We were in there last night for midnight mass. It was the first time we had been back in the place since the ill-fated 'altar boys' disaster, a few months ago.

Tom and his family were there, and it was a great excuse for staying up really late. Mr Thomas, the vicar, had been droning on about something or other, whilst me and Tom had been quietly arguing about what kills the man in the Ferrari at the start of the film 'The Italian Job.' Tom says, the man in the car crashes it into the JCB (or the Italian equivalent) that must have been parked in the tunnel. I reckon it was a bomb that blows up the pretty red car, whatever. In the background, Mr Thomas was reading something from the bible about having to give up childish ways when you get older. That would be sad I thought to myself.

Back to Christmas day, wet and bruised but happy, so happy, I say goodbye to Tom, and me and Neil tuck our (not so new) dirty skateboards under our arms and head in for turkey.

Chapter 24

I think I might be going a bit crazy. We are three weeks into this grim event but it feels like three life times.

Work have told me that I'm on 'carer's leave' and they are being fantastic but I couldn't care less about work. I'm beginning to not function very well. I'm moody with Louise and sometimes impatient with the nurses and doctors when they hurt my little girl, but they can't help it and they don't do it on purpose. They didn't invent the drug Vincristine, which stings like hell when it is injected into her. It's not their fault that they haven't invented a more comfortable way of shoving a tube down her nose. It isn't their fault that chemotherapy makes her puke all day and all night.

There is a pram that has ward thirty-one scrawled on it in white pen, but it has ended up here on ward thirty-four. Emma lies in it most days and sleeps in it at night. She can't settle in her bed.

She needed a blood transfusion today. Seems horrifying but apparently it's not unusual. It will be the first of many they have said. The chemo' drugs have wreaked havoc with her red blood cells. When one of the numerous daily blood tests indicated that her count was getting seriously low, they attached a sack of blood onto the metal stand, next to her antibiotic drip, and connected it via a tube into the cannula in her hand. Her other blood cells and platelets will also need topping up, if they are to keep her alive.

Still no news on the 'Philadelphia' test yet, which adds to my fears. It seems the Americans are too busy fighting their war to test my daughter's chromosomes.

Billy, Alice, Jordon, Matthew, Allister. These are some of the other regular inmates on the ward. All going through the same horrors, as the world outside the hospital carries on oblivious. I look out of the dirty, rain splattered window in our room. Bristol rush hour traffic crawls by, like time.

Chapter 25

Electric Fishing

"**B**right eyes, burning like fire.
Bright eyes, how could they close and fail?"

Not Art Garfunkel's voice, but a boy, younger than me, dressed as a brown bunny rabbit, holding a carrot, hilariously murdering the title song from the film 'Watership Down' on Tiswas, with Chris Tarrant and Sally James. I really, really like Sally James off Tiswas. There, I've said it, no more talk of that.

It's Saturday lunchtime, April 1979. Today, is electric fishing day. If you've never been electric fishing, you really have missed out. All you need for electric fishing is:-

1. A river
2. Electricity
3. A boat shaped like a bath tub but slightly bigger
4. Some grown-ups in rubber waders and rubber gloves.

It's been foggy, but the mist around the river Evenlode has lifted now. Me, Tom, Neil and a handful of other lads from school, make our way over the huge 'Dean Taylor bridge' and down the steep track, where me and Tom nearly killed ourselves on his mum's bike a couple of years ago.

We head right, passed Bridge Cottage and over the river bridge (that we hang jam jars off in the summer to catch minnows). In the middle of the narrow river, about twenty-five yards downstream from the bridge, is a small boat, with three men in it: two are standing, one is sitting on a plank. They are all wearing life jackets (though the river isn't very deep), rubber waders and gloves, so the boat looks a bit cramped. One of the men, who is standing up, has a strange looking device in his hand that resembles something like a small TV aerial, attached to a pole that is about five feet long. I can see the TV aerial thing has a cable attached to it that runs down the pole and into the boat. The other man, who is standing up, also has a pole, but this one is longer and it has a large net on the end of it.

The sun is breaking through the last of the mist as we run along the riverbank and catch up with the boat. The grass in the meadow is wet and I am glad I put my wellies on. We quickly catch up to the boat, which is drifting slowly downstream in the current. The man sat down on the plank has a small ore and is gently steering the boat when necessary.

This small stretch of the river Evenlode is pretty special. Why else would silly men, in a silly boat, with silly things in their hands be here if it wasn't? You see, there is a mile stretch of this river which is prime for trout fishing. It is almost impossible to get a permit to fish this stretch of the river. The only way you can get one is if you've got about a million pounds, know someone very famous or have a tweed jacket. We don't have any of these things. We do fish the other parts of the river, for chub and dace, but for some reason, you only catch trout in this prime mile stretch. It's like the trout know they are not allowed to swim outside this exclusive band of water.

A gamekeeper is employed all year round to stop people poaching trout. Neil, my brother, is the only person I know to have successfully poached two brown trout out of this stretch. He did it really early one morning last summer, catching the 'brownies' on worms, one cast after the other. They were about three quarters of a pound each, and he held them by the tail and whacked them over his size six welly boots. They died instantly and he took them back home, gutted them in the kitchen sink and mum cooked them. She wasn't particularly impressed that he had poached them, but she didn't see the point in wasting them. They tasted bloody lovely. He was lucky he hadn't got caught; he would have been flogged in public (or something worse) if he had.

Anyway, that is the reason why the men are in the boat, because of the precious trout. They are taking out the predators from the water, the pike, so that they don't eat all the 'brownies.' The TV aerial thing puts an electrical current in the water, just enough to stun all the fish within about a ten feet circle of the charge.

Around the boat now, slowly but surely, we start to see fish, all dazed and bellies up, floating to the surface: gudgeon, roach, dace, chub, minnows, trout. It is so exciting. Let's face it, it isn't everyday you see loads of fish on the surface of this murky, green river. More gudgeon, then a big chub (a couple of pounds) bobs up to the surface. A beautiful stripy perch lolls on its side near the bank. The perch is also a predator, but this one is only small; it's the pike they're after. No signs yet. The stunned fish soon gather their senses and with a flash, they right themselves, spin around and dive back into the depths.

We follow the boat a further fifty yards downstream. A larger group of spectators have joined us boys, and are watching the man with the net, peering into the gloomy waters, looking to scoop out a long, muscular, unconscious pike. Still no sign. I've only ever seen one pike before; it was dead in some reeds further upstream. It was about three pounds and a foot and a bit long. Me and Tom poked it with a stick. I could see the rows of razor sharp teeth in its gaping mouth. It made me shudder and the smell of death made me feel a bit sick.

"There!" Neil shouts, pointing directly down into the water, four feet below our boots on the edge of the bank. Surfacing, like a scaly submarine, the torpedo shaped pike rolls on the surface, disorientated, and in a flash, the man in the boat scoops up the hapless fish. The pole bends under the weight of the six or seven pound monster. It is rudely dumped into a black, plastic dustbin on the boat with a splash. I feel exhilarated and sad at the same time as I watch this strange activity playing out in front of me.

After an hour or so, the boat has reached the end of the exclusive stretch of water and four pike splash around the dustbin. The men come ashore and tie the boat up. They don't say much when they haul the black bin out onto the bank. I don't want to see them kill the pike, so me and Tom start to head back.

When Neil catches us up, fifteen minutes later, we are nearing Tom's house. Slung over his shoulder is the pike he had pointed to earlier.

"Mum's gunna kill you." I say.

"I know, but I had to get a closer look at it," he replies. Neil loves his fish and fishing. He wouldn't have killed this pike if he had caught it on a line, he would have let it go, let it get bigger, as they don't taste anywhere near as good as brown trout. But this pike was doomed the moment it got electrocuted. But now it was dead, Neil was fascinated in seeing what it looked like close up. Trouble is, there is no way mum was going to gut and cook this monster and she will end up having to dispose of it somehow.

Neil gently laid the fish down onto the grass verge. I looked into its cold, faded black eye, down its beautifully camouflaged flank, touched (with my finger), its strong, spiky, red dorsal fin and powerful tail. Its head and jaws took up about a third of its overall length. It was magnificent, no doubt; but mum was still going to kill him.

Chapter 26

Diary: 12.30am Monday 23rd or 24th March 2003

I 'm not sure why I'm doing this, but I just need to write down what I'm thinking. It's about half past midnight on Monday morning. I'm not sure what the date is but I guess it's the 23rd or 24th March 2003.

The last week has been pretty much unspeakable. I don't know whether I intend this to be the start of Emma's A.L.L. diary or what. Part of me hopes not but a bit of me hopes it will be.

I keep getting these waves of horrible, fatal feelings, that I just know there isn't going to be a happy ending to this. My greatest sadness will be that Emma goes through all this pain and doesn't make it. There is another pain though, my pain. I'm not sure if I can deal with not knowing the outcome, the uncertainty is killing me. If I'm being selfish, thinking about myself, well, I can't help it.

I've made plans in my head about the funeral and memorial gardens. Part of me thinks I'm too fatalistic, but the other part thinks I have to prepare myself.

Louise is so positive and level headed about all this, it is almost untrue. I wouldn't change her outlook and it's how she deals with it, but I sometimes find it difficult, her being so laid back.

My little darling has been a bit better today than yesterday. She's got a bug but her temps down and tomorrow they might put in the Hickman line or long line or 'wiggly' line, whatever they call it.

I've read some stuff on A.L.L. today and Holly the nurse went through it all. I've been reluctant to read anything about it and I'm not sure if I'm ready yet to go into it in great detail. I'm not sure I ever want to.

Dr. Jim keeps being positive and so far he has been by far the best at keeping me from thinking the worst. However, the worst isn't far from my mind most of the time. I hear Dr. Jim speaking positively to all the kids and their parents on the ward, but I know some of them will die, won't they?

I did read some statistics in a yellow booklet just before I came to bed tonight. Looks like Professor Elmwood was right when he said Emma's chances of getting this was about 1:50,000. How the fuck can that be? It's not fair, she doesn't deserve it and I don't think I do either.

I still feel like it is all a bit of a dream. A surreal nightmare. Maybe if I can write something down when I feel like crying (which is about everyday at the moment), it might make things easier for me. Sounds selfish again.

Alex is being great but I'm starting to think I need to go back home with him the next time he comes here. Even now I feel my thoughts aren't really with him as much as I would like, but I just haven't got the strength at the moment.

I'd probably normally read over this and check it for spelling and grammar mistakes, because I'm normally pretty bad, but I'm not going to, no one's gunna read it accept me anyway.

Good night my darling.

I'll probably do this a lot. Stop writing and then remember what I was going to put down in the first place. Although Emma was a bit better today, she was moody, but she did do her 'lion's roar' for me, 'raaaah!!' She also touched her tummy when I asked her to and yesterday she gave her dad a kiss.

I carried her around in my left arm today, pushing her drip with my right hand. I think she kinda likes that, although when we go into a room that she pointed at, when she gets there she moans and wriggles and points to another room.

Good night again my darling.

[I did read it all through for spelling and grammar. Good job too, it was embarrassingly riddled with errors!]

Chapter 27

May Day

It's seven thirty in the morning on May 1st 1979. May Day. Thirty children from Lambe primary school (that's half the school), are in the wood, just out the back of the playing field, quietly picking bluebells and cowslips. The early morning, mid spring sun, is penetrating the leaf canopy and shards of yellow light are acting as theatre spot lights, lighting up this fairy tale scene amongst the trees.

There are so many bluebells, the floor of the wood is a sweet smelling carpet of blue. Mr Walker, Mrs Webster and my mum are the only teachers at the school and they are all here this morning, with buckets, dozens of them.

May Day is a big event in Lambe, as it is in many villages around Oxfordshire; possibly around the world as far as I know. The flowers are an essential ingredient in this festival: they will decorate the school, all the girls will have flowers in their hair, the teachers will have flowers in their hair, the crown of the Maypole will be covered, and most importantly, the May carriage will be completely in bloom.

The May carriage is basically a chariot, and sitting in it for almost all of the day will be the May Queen. The May Queen is voted for by the children in the school, a few weeks before the big event. The Queen is always a girl in her final year at primary school; the year in which she will move to big school, with all the hopes and excitement that brings. This year's Queen is Jessica Wakeman. She is the prettiest girl in my class and one of the quietist. Slim, funny, full of life; with shiny dark hair and brown eyes.

May Queens need a May King, and this year, it's me. There

are only seven boys in my year, and we are all fools, so I am not sure how I got more votes than the others, but I did. Tom is my deputy King for the day, because I chose him. He will have to wear a green smock, whereas I will be wearing a velvet cloak and a gold crown (which looks like Daniel Dravot's in 'The Man Who Would Be King.' Cool - although I hope I don't get chucked off 'Dean Taylor's bridge' for being an imposter!).

Once the enormous amount of flowers have been picked, they are bunched and put in the water buckets and everyone heads back to school. The May carriage sits, bare, in Mr Walker's garage. The garage doors are opened and Mr Walker, Mrs Webster, my mum and about ten kids (I am one of them), lug in the buckets of flowers; the garage doors are closed behind us.

After about an hour, around nine o'clock, the doors are opened and the carriage has been transformed from an ugly duckling into a beautiful swan (though it's mostly blue and yellow, not white!). Even as an eleven year old boy - who mostly couldn't care less about flowers - I think it's impressive, it looks magnificent in fact; fit for a Queen. I do get to sit in it for a bit, but mostly I have to push the bloody thing around the village, with Tom and a couple of the other boys in my class, for about three hours.

But first there is an assembly in the school where all the parents are allowed to attend. Me and Jessica Wakeman are sat on thrones on the stage, the thrones are covered in flowers and the scent is almost overpowering. The small hall is packed and everyone is standing and singing the hymn, 'Morning Has Broken.' My mum is playing the piano, quite badly.

After the assembly, we make our way out onto the playground where our chariot awaits. I climb in, and then realise that I should have let my Queen go in first, but it's too late to reverse out and my cloak is caught on something. Jessica doesn't mind anyway and she elegantly gets in, looking lovely in a white, Queen like dress; a tiara of cowslips on her head.

For most of the morning we push the smart chariot around the village, collecting money in the buckets, which had been used as temporary vases for all the flowers earlier in the day. Once that is done, everyone goes home for their lunch, and then assemble on The Green at about two o'clock for the main event; Maypole dancing. Maypole dancing isn't a sport, but we treat it as such. You are not actually competing against anyone else, it is simply that your school year wants to make less mistakes than the year before. These are the unwritten rules of Maypole dancing for competitive eleven year olds, and everyone knows it.

Last year, Neil, my brother, was pipped to May Day royalty by his best mate, Stephen 'Welly' Wilkins; so he was obviously unimpressed that I had gone one better this year. His class only made one mistake in 1978, it was an almost flawless performance, almost. Seven dances: ranging from the relatively simple 'Barber's Pole', to the immensely complicated 'Spider's Web' and 'Gypsy's Tent.' And, it was in the final unravelling of the 'Gypsy's Tent'' last year, that Malcolm Crockford had gone under when he should have gone over, and the whole dance came to a shuddering halt. The circle of parents clapped, but not as loudly as they would have following a perfect show. The accordion player had hung his head in disappointment. Maypole dancing was pressure, real pressure.

But that was last year, now it was our turn. Our first five dances go without a hitch, the applause grew louder after each performance. Even my dad has taken the day off as an 'agent,' to watch his little lad prancing around in a cape and a pair of black plimsolls.

The 'Spider's Web' dance had been a disaster in rehearsals; Claire Franklin had nearly been strangled to death and had to be unwound, sobbing, by Mr Walker.

The 'Spider's Web' was the second to last dance, and it was a tense affair, but we somehow pulled it off. The crowd roared. The boys from last year, including my brother, looked on, grim faced, arms folded tightly across their chests, hoping for a mistake, just the smallest error. Everyone else started clapping and stamping their feet, as the fiddle player ramped it up for the finale, the 'Gypsy's Tent.'

I looked at my partner, Jessica, my Queen, and we gave each other a good luck stare. All around the Maypole, the other couples were doing the same. And then we were off: under, over, under, over, twisting and turning, the pattern of the ribbons making a spectacular roof to the 'Gypsy's Tent.' Around and around we go, in and out, in and out, nearly there now; just need to retrace our steps and unravel this magnificent structure. The music grows to a crescendo, the dancers are in stern concentration, blocking out the noise of the vast crowd; we pass the point where Malcolm Crockford cocked it up last year; nearly there, nearly... and then suddenly, out of the corner of my eye, three dancing partners along, I see Wayne Harper skidding to halt. His partner Lisa Davis, tries to keep him going, and then suddenly pushes away his hands, screams and she runs off into the crowd. The other pairs of dancers behind him can't stop in time and everyone is running into the back of each other, slipping over. The fiddle player lowers his bow, the accordion player is shaking his head for the second time in two years. The crowd is deathly quiet.

Wayne Harper is stood, frozen to the spot, about ten feet away from me. Most of the other dancers, including me and my Queen, have slipped or been bundled to the muddy ground. My crown is laying in the dirt, crumpled. Panting and not believing what has just happened, we all look up at Wayne; his arms stretched out, hands pointing up, fingers splayed. "Oh Christ," he cries, "I've shat myself!"

As the crowds drifted away, disappointed eleven year olds dusted themselves off. Wayne had been whisked away by his mum to their house on Woodstock Street, to be hosed down in the bath. He would be embarrassed forever, I guessed, but I wouldn't ever mention it to him, he was a good lad.

I stood on The Green with Tom by a trestle table that had some half-drunk cups of squash on it. I still had my robe on, but my crown was irreparable and in the bin. Tom put his cup of orange squash down. "You know Wayne's had the shits all week," he said seriously.

"Yeah, I know," I replied, and we both start laughing as we watch my mum, the other teachers and some parents tidying away the sorry May Day scene.

Chapter 28

Diary: 10.30pm Tuesday 25th March 2003

A   *really bad morning and early afternoon but a better evening. Still very down when I got up and didn't get to the hospital until about 11am. Emma didn't have her 'wiggly' long line put in because of her infection, but they did do her lumber puncture (LP) under general anaesthetic at 1.30pm.*

So she couldn't drink or eat all morning. It was quite (no very!) upsetting to see her so distressed. After the LP she was OK and ate 2 rounds of toast and jam in about 30 seconds flat. She perked up late afternoon, doing loads of 'lion roars' for me and some 'crocodile teeth gnashing'. She's getting very good at it!

Claire, a nurse from ward 35, was really good all day and gave Emma her last of the day antibiotic injection at 7.30pm. For once Emma didn't notice that the nurse was doing it, as she played with my glasses as we laid on the bed together.

Prof. Elmwood felt her tum this morning and said she was, "A bit gassy." I'm kinda feeling a bit brighter tonight, although I have this bad feeling that we're going to get told something is not going to plan really soon.

Awaiting this bloody chromosome test is worrying me as well.

I reckon I'll go back home with Alex tomorrow for the night. I'm looking forward to that.

Good night my darling.

Diary: Friday 28th March 2003

I didn't write anything the last couple of days because I spent Wednesday night back home with Alex. It was lovely to take him to bed and to wake up with him. I took him to school the following day for the first time ever and I was happy with the way he settled down at his table when I took him in.

Even now I'm getting all the days mixed up.

Anyway, today is Friday. We had some better news. The 'bad chromosome' test (or the 'Philadelphia' test) was negative! Dr. Jim gave us the good news at about 2pm and my heart was the lightest it's been for a couple of weeks.

We took Emma for a walk in her pushchair down by the docks and I got a little fussy about it being too cold.

I promised myself a little drinkie if the chromosome test was OK, so I had a bottle of Stella that Louise's dad had brought up and left in the Clic house fridge last week. Of course, I think that celebrating this small victory against the relentless cancer will only bring bad luck later on, but I can't stop myself (thinking like this).

Alex is coming with Louise's mum and dad tomorrow.

Emma did her 'lion's roar' before I left for Clic house tonight. I sang her 'Two Little Boys' and 'Incy Wincey Spider.'

Good night my darling.

Diary: Sunday 30th March 2003.

Just really worried and scared.

Good night my darling.

Diary: Tuesday 1st April 2003.

In the hospital last night. Had about 3-4 hours' sleep. Not all Emma keeping me awake (although her poo is really bad). I just can't sleep properly at the moment. Prof. Elmwood, Dr. Jim, Jo the S.H.O and Holly the nurse, all paid a visit to say she is doing OK and her low blood counts shouldn't cause a bone marrow test delay next week.

Emma's infection and bum virus means she can't have her 'wiggly' line in on Thursday though. No matter.

Emma hasn't left the ward 31 pram for about 3 days. She lives in that rather than her bed, or my arms. She must find some sanctuary and peace in it. She's pale and tired but she did the odd turn of 'head dancing' today with a little, weak smile on her face.

Holly, the nurse, was really nice and attentive all day, as we are quarantined in our side room.

Neil phoned me (as he has done everyday) and asked me to give Emma a kiss from him. I forgot. I'll do it tomorrow.

I kinda feel like I've reached the point where I've accepted that she has leukaemia and I need to deal with it.

Back in Clic house tonight there are parents who, I think, have just found out about their little one's plight. This means they found out after us. It makes me feel like a veteran already, and I'm only in the 4th week of my 'tour.'

Spoke to Billy's mum in the kitchen tonight, but it's hard to either offer support or feel supported, because the cancers the kids have on the

143

ward are all so different. You only understand your child's illness. The only thing you have in common is the horror of it all.

I'm sure I've mentioned it before but mum, dad, Neil and Louise's mum and dad have all been wonderful.

Dear Alex

I'm sorry we're not with you to cuddle you, especially because you are not feeling well today. I hope you understand all this one day, better still, not remember any of it.

We love you dearly.

Love Dad

Ps Good night my darlings.

Diary: Thursday 3rd April 2003.

OK. A better day today. Dr. Jim confirmed that Emma is considered a 'lower risk' (of relapse?) because of her age, her sex, her chromosome test result and because of the relatively low number of leukaemia cells in her, when she was diagnosed. The thing I'm not sure about though, is if she doesn't show quick remission signs (from her imminent, first bone marrow test next week), will this 'lower risk' status change?

I'm trying to think one stage at a time but as soon as I get good news, I'm moving onto the next bad scenario.

Alex is much better from his cold and we saw him yesterday. We couldn't take him to see Emma 'cos she is still infectious from the Norwalk virus. He seemed to me the exact opposite of Emma – rosy cheeks, smiley face and dark complexion. Made me dead happy to see him.

We (Louise and me) took Alex around Bristol docks and the river all afternoon as Louise's mum stayed with Emma.

Emma's bum seems a bit better. Pretty Nurse Kate, the Sister, was really nice (we had our first real chat today). She told me that if all goes well, Emma will not remember a thing about this when she is older. God, I hope so. But then there is the, "if all goes well," to contend with first….

Got my hair cut today and by coincidence saw Nurse Kate in the hairdressers — she had fallen over and twisted an ankle. Why had she done that? I need all Emma's doctors and nurses to be fit and healthy. Talking of which I thought Prof. Elmwood looked a bit under the weather today.

Charlotte, who I work with, texted me tonight. Really good to hear from her. Mike, my mate from work is coming up to see me tomorrow. Looking forward to that.

Dr. Jim and Nurse David did Emma's Vincristine injection this evening. This is the one that will make her hair fall out. No sign of that yet. Strange.

Good night my darling.

Diary: Saturday 5th April 2003

My little darling, wearing her 'Daddy's Girl' T-shirt, had her little pink boots on and walked about 4-5 steps in our side room today. First time she's really been out of her ward 31 pram in a week!

She is still v. weak and pale though. Lovely day and we were allowed to take Emma to the park. We all had a nice time and I guess Emma appreciated a change of scene. I know I did.

Yesterday my friend Mike came to see me. Lovely day, really good to see him. Had a couple of pints sitting on the quay outside the Arnolfini in Bristol docks. I did the same with my brother Neil last Sunday, which was equally distracting.

Next Tuesday is going to be a big day in all this. I hope it goes well.

I'm writing this at 11pm and I shall watch the Brazilian Grand Prix qualifying in an hour.

Good night my darling.

Diary: Monday 7th April 2003

Last night it was my turn on 'Emma watch' at the hospital. And I did just that during the adverts of the film 'The Perfect Storm,' I watched her. Asleep in her pram, head tilted towards the bed, beautiful, pointy little chin, small mouth, almost transparent eye lids, pale skin, the TV flashing different colours across her face. Clockwise golden curls laying on her forehead. Beautiful, beautiful little girl.

A delicate kiss on her cheek. Good night my darling.

Diary: Tuesday 8th April 2003

Emma had her first bone marrow test today. Result in 1-2 days. Everything crossed. She had the test under general anaesthetic when they also did her lumber puncture injection (the one that puts chemo' into her spinal column!).

Her poos are a bit better again and she is off the antibiotics.

Dr. Joanne got a smile off Emma today, which is more than I got.

Saddam Hussain is dead they think.

Had a great day yesterday with Alex at Clic house. Mum and dad had brought him in and we played Frisbee in the garden.

Good night my darling.

Chapter 29

The Fire

Cricket up the drive at Catterpie Cottage is excellent, no doubts about that. But cricket on the school field, when you have broken up for the summer holidays, is something else.

It is the last summer holidays until we go off to big school. St. Matthew's school Craveley is where we are going; me and Tom. But that's ages away, it's July 1979, and we've got the whole of the summer holidays to enjoy.

No windows to break playing cricket here fortunately. Although a mammoth hit would get the ball somewhere near to Tom's house (that overlooks the school playing fields), there is little danger of eleven year olds hitting a hard cricket ball that far. Because we are going to play a lot of cricket on this field during the summer holidays, me and Tom are going to do it properly. We are going to mow out a cricket strip with Tom's dad's lawn mower; it's one of those old pushy ones where you can see the blades spin around. We drag the mower out of Tom's garage: passed the Battle Wagon and his mum's bike, then roll it down the drive, over the road and haul it over the small, stone wall that surrounds the school field.

We decide on the flattest bit of ground: down the far end of the field, near the PE shed, and cut the already well cropped grass a little bit shorter. After fifteen minutes we have a perfect (if a little green), rectangular 'Test Match' wicket. The stumps, where the batsman will bat, are in front of a five feet high, plastic mesh fence, which separates the playing fields from the allotments behind. My dad used to have an allotment here (well, half an allotment, because he shared it with Harry Fairbrother, the fire eating lawyer and our next door neighbour). I think they quite liked the idea of growing their own veg', but they soon realised that it takes loads of time and effort and they both had jobs in London. Having caught the Kenbury to Paddington train at six thirty in the morning, when they got back home at seven thirty at night, quite frankly they couldn't be arsed to go digging. So they gave it up. By the time they decided to jack it in, dad and Harry's allotment was a weed jungle, full of slugs. The professional allotment keepers of Lambe, probably weren't too happy at having this wasteland next to their pristine market gardens; with their fussy rows of fruit and veg'. I think dad and Harry grew about ten potatoes and some sorry runner beans before they decided to bail out.

Anyway, this fence obviously stops our cricket ball from going into the allotments, but it also acts as wicketkeeper and slip fielders. We push Tom's dad's mower out of the way (I have no idea how he cuts his massive lawn with this thing!), set the stumps up and I prepare to bat. Neil has just pulled up on his Chopper, so we will have a three way game - all against all, the most runs wins. This will probably last until teatime (with a little break for lunch). It's eleven o'clock now; the time that all 'Test Matches' start.

The day is hot already and by lunchtime we have all had a couple of bats each. We don't wear pads or gloves, because we don't have any; we do play with a proper hard cricket ball though, because it is more fun than a tennis ball. We have one bat between us, it is mine, and written in blue ballpoint pen on the shoulder of this bat, it says 'Do not use hard ball.' No matter, it hasn't broken yet.

It's about twelve thirty and 'Welly', Neil's friend, has joined us. He is fielding by the wall, Neil is bowling, Tom's by the PE shed on the leg side and I am batting. I've scored 16 runs and have just hit Neil for a 'four' through the covers.

David Gower would have been proud.

Just as Neil steams in to bowl again, doing his impersonation of Bob Willis, 'Welly' shouts something from the boundary. I think it was, "Fucking hell!", but it could have been, "Jesus Christ!" Either way, I drop the bat and we all run to the wall where 'Welly' has a perfect view of the village road, which runs up from the river and passed Tom's house and the school.

What 'Welly' has seen is extraordinary, scary and exciting. A tractor is coming up the road, towing a trailer full of hay, and the back half of the trailer is completely on fire! By the time the tractor and trailer reach us, we can see that the driver of the tractor is Eddy Macy (the dad of one of the younger kids in the school), and for some reason he has clearly not noticed that he is towing a bonfire. As the tractor and flaming trailer slowly drives passed, all four of us are now stood on the stone wall, shouting and waving at Mr Macy, and pointing to the scene of potential disaster right behind him.

Now, Eddy Macy is an enormous man and I can only assume that his neck is so fat that he couldn't turn it to look in his mirrors, because unbelievably the tractor rumbles by, sparks and flames bellowing off the back of the trailer. We notice that three boys on bikes are following this weirdness, and also waving at the driver. Finally, Eddy seems to acknowledge that his payload, tractor and his life are in serious danger, so he heaves his massive body off the seat in an attempt to turn around and see what is happening. At last, he realises that the situation is more than serious and stops the tractor just around the corner from Tom's house.

We all jump off the wall and catch up with the blaze, which has really taken hold now. The twenty feet, flat bed, wooden and metal trailer is packed, ten feet high with hay and now the whole thing is alight. We can't get too close because of the heat and stand a decent way back; but even then the intensity of the fire is absolutely amazing. Eddy has clambered out of the cab now, red in the face and huffing and puffing in a dirty blue boiler suit, muddy wellies and a flat cap. He hasn't got time to uncouple the tractor from the trailer and so the fuel in the tank is a serious problem now.

The boys on the bikes have also stopped and a few people have come out to see what the hell has been driven into their village. We stand open mouthed, as the flames start to melt the tyres of the trailer. Tom's mum runs around the corner. She had called the fire brigade as soon as she saw it drive passed her house. They would be coming from Woodstock, about ten minutes away. Less with their lights and nee-nors on!

Bang! One of the tyres goes. Everyone takes a step back. The back window of the cab in the tractor shatters. The flames are nearly as high as the surrounding roofs of the houses now; this is going to get messy. But just in time two fire engines scream around the corner. The firemen jump out and set about quickly and efficiently putting out the blaze. One of the firemen is talking to Eddy, who is looking a bit shocked, and is pointing towards the three boys on their bikes.

It takes a surprisingly short time to put out the fire. The tractor is just about in one piece, a little scorched but the trailer is completely burnt out. All that is left is the metal frame and piled on top of the axle, is a big, smoky heap of wet embers.

Me, Tom, Neil and 'Welly' realised that we haven't spoken at all whilst this has been going on; we'd just stared. Cricket had been fun, but this had been something else. Neil pointed above the smouldering mess, and we all looked up together to see that the telegraph wires, which had been stretched out above the fire had melted, and they now hung down off their poles, like black tentacles.

The day after, we went back to the field to finish off our game of cricket. But before we did so, the four of us walked around to where the fire had been put out. The tractor and trailer had been tidied away, but on the tarmac was a big black stain and bits of burnt hay fluttered around in the breeze.

As we walked back towards the school field, Tom says, "D'you see those boys on bikes who followed the tractor up yesterday?"

"Yes," we all reply, turning to Tom.

"Well, I heard that Eddy Macy reckons they chucked a match onto the back of the trailer and that's what set it alight."

"Humm," we mumble, nodding.

Tom continued, "But when the police talked to them, they said it was a spark from the exhaust pipe. Anyway, I reckon those boys were from Stonesford."

"Yeah," we say in unison.

Chapter 30

Diary: Thursday 10 April 2003

Y*esterday we got the first bone marrow test result. It was A-OK. Not sure what it really means in the long-term but well pleased. The blood doctors got the result a day early which was great. There is another super important bone marrow test in a few weeks that is really critical.*

Dr. Jim discussed the research aspects of leukaemia today. He gave us some information to read and some forms to sign to confirm we were happy that the details of Emma's cancer 'journey' are fed into a medical database to help future research efforts. I find it difficult to believe that some parents would not sign it, but not all do apparently. We signed.

It's kind of 'so far so good,' I guess, in terms of the initial tests isn't it? She's 'lower risk' of something (relapse?) and her initial remission was quick. But the majority of kids diagnosed with A.L.L are lower risk and 95% have quick remission. But still 25% of them DIE!! I knew I shouldn't have read that fucking booklet.

I want to ask whether Emma's chances of survival have now been pushed up beyond the 75% mark with these positive (well negative, technically) test results.

The booklet says that the majority of children who relapse are from the initial lower risk group – I guess that is because most are in that low risk group. Oh Christ, I don't know, it's not quite adding up.

Anyway, as Alice's dad said to me a few days ago (when I started this stupid statistics conversation with him in the Clic house kitchen), "They either live 100% or they don't," he'd said. He is right, of course, although I wonder if he does think about what Alice's chances really are.

We might get home tomorrow. Emma is off her saline drip but I don't think she is drinking enough by herself yet to be released. By going home, of course, I mean staying in our room at Clic house, not our real house, our lovely comfortable home in the Forest. That's way off.

It would be great though if we could get her out of the hospital for a couple of nights, because next Thursday it is planned that she will have her operation to put in her long line, her Hickman line, her 'wiggly' (call it what you like). She will, no doubt, have huge infections following that operation, so to get her out of the place now would be marvellous.

Anyway, after yesterday's good news regarding the first bone marrow result, I felt pretty shit all day. I think I'm tired from being up every 30 minutes with Emma (she is grisly and doesn't know what she wants, love her – it's the steroids they say). But I think I was a bit angry today as well. Like I've done the grieving bit and today I was just angry. I can imagine a 'Shrink' pointing to some pictures in a circle, joined up with arrows depicting the cycle of emotions you go through with something like this. They've got it right so far.

So, I'm angry and maybe I'm bored too. The days and nights are endless, gut retching, tediously long stretches in a clinical, macabre world.

I've just had a bath back at Clic house and my friend Simon has just left a message on my phone; hadn't heard from him in ages, it was nice of him.

An image of my old mate, Tom Tate, flickered through my mind today. He had a big smile on his big face.

I found out today that Jordon, on our ward, has A.L.L. He's 18 months old (the same age as Emma) and he looks really well! That's a good sign, right? Jordon's dad is really positive and he seems typical of most of the parents I've spoken to. I'm not sure I can be like that. I feel I need to suffer with her. Stupid I know!

People say, "Where were you when JFK got shot?" Well, I wasn't born until '68, so it's irrelevant to me, but I wonder if they will say in the future:-

"Can you remember where were you when those American soldiers pulled down that Statue of Saddam in Iraq, and stupidly draped the 'Stars and Stripes' all over it?" I could reply to that one. "Yes," I'd say, "I was in side room 1, ward 34, paediatric oncology unit, Bristol children's hospital, watching it on the fucking telly!"

Good night my darling, hope we can get you out of hospital for one night tomorrow.

Chapter 31

Grand Prix

I Am a very lucky little lad. My dad is taking me, my brother, and my mum to the British Grand Prix at Silverstone. He also took us two years ago in 1977, where we watched James Hunt in the McLaren beat John Watson in the Alfa Romeo. I like James Hunt, he's pretty cool, but he wasn't driving a Ferrari, so I didn't really care whether he won or not. I had wanted his main rival, Niki Lauda, the Austrian, to win driving the pretty red car from Maranello in Northern Italy. You see I am a proper little tifosi, a Ferrari fan. We tifosi don't care if Italians drive our cars or not; it's the car that counts when you are a Ferrari fan.

Although James Hunt won the British Grand Prix two years ago, Niki won the World Championship for the second time in three years. But Lauda doesn't drive a Ferrari anymore, the scarlet cars are piloted by Jody Scheckter and the little French Canadian, Gilles Villeneuve, and it is these two names that I have painted on an old white sheet my mum gave me. Yes, I've made a banner. It isn't as big as the ones I've seen the fans make for the Italian Grand Prix, which hang off the stands in Monza, but it's pretty big. I've painted the Ferrari badge: a yellow shield, with a black prancing horse in the middle of it. It has the initials S and F on the shield, which stands for Scuderia Ferrari – it means the Ferrari Stable. I know that, because I read it in AutoSport, the motor racing magazine that my dad sometimes buys during the motor racing season.

Dad, sometimes, also buys the pink Italian sports paper Gazzetta Dello Sport. He says you can only buy it in London, which is useful because he goes to work there everyday on the train. He gets this paper out of his briefcase when he gets home from work and gives it to me. I can't understand any of it, but it's full of pictures of Jody and Gilles and their Ferrari 312T4. I cut them out and put them on my wall, next to my massive, coloured poster of Villeneuve, sliding his Ferrari around a corner at the South African Grand Prix.

We had to get up at half past five this morning. There was a knock at the door at six o'clock and my mum and dad's friends are standing there. Annie and Bev are a super cool couple, a bit younger than my mum and dad. Bev is wearing a pair of tiny denim shorts, a white T-shirt with a black and gold John Player Special Lotus Formula One car on it. Annie has a white summer skirt on and a blue, strappy top. I like Annie, OK, I do. They are both wearing sunglasses.

"Are you ready?" They say to me as I open the door.

"You bet," I reply and me and mum carry some blankets and cushions out to their car. Bev and Annie drive a black Alfa Romeo; of course they do.

My newly painted Ferrari banner is neatly folded and sits next to our packed lunches in a large padded bag, which sits on top a number of metal poles and wooden planks; which fill the back of a small white and orange van, which is being driven by my dad. My mum is sat next to dad and on the side of the van it says 'Thomas Cook.' Dad would normally be driving his Lancia Beta Coupe 2000 (which is equally as cool as Annie and Bev's Alfa Romeo), but he has this van today because he can't fit the builder's scaffolding poles in the boot of his handsome, blue Italian car.

***

Me and Neil (asleep) are in the back of Annie and Bev's Alfa and we are now parked in a layby, just outside the town of

Woodstock, behind the van that my dad has borrowed from work. We only left home about twenty minutes ago.

"Excuse me, sir, but can I ask, why do you have scaffolding poles and such like equipment in the back of this 'Thomas Cook' van?" asks the uniformed policemen, with what looks like a raygun in his right hand. This is a pretty reasonable question, I guess; it does look a bit unusual, but it is not as if my dad is about to do a bank job or anything, not with my mum anyway, who is sat next to him, looking down and shaking her head slightly.

"We are going to Silverstone, to watch the Grand Prix, and we build this small scaffolding platform and sit on it." My dad offers the policemen as an explanation.

"And, who are the "we", sir, if you don't mind me asking?" The policemen interrogates further, looking at the red figures on the display of his raygun.

"My wife and I, and my two children and our friends who are in that black Alfa parked up behind us, talking to your colleague and presumably being booked for speeding as well."

"Oh, I see, sir, that's all fine then. Luckily though, your friends behind you weren't speeding, but unfortunately, you were. Thirty-four miles an hour in a 'thirty' is pretty dangerous, sir. You will receive a letter within the next few days." The policemen scribbles something down on a pad and hands it to my dad through the window of the van. "Have a good day at the Grand Prix, sir," the rozzer concludes, and waves dad's smoky van and our sporty Alfa on their way.

My dad was clearly fed up that he had been done for speeding, but he wasn't going to let it spoil his day, and it certainly wasn't going to spoil mine. As we get close to

Silverstone, on one of the small approach roads, I can see part of the track. Excitement immediately grows in my tum. I recognise this section of tarmac, it's the short, downhill straight between Stowe and Club corners, which is exactly where we will be heading and where we will be setting up our 'viewing platform.'

It takes about an hour to queue to get into the circuit, but we sit patiently in the car; Abba's Voulez-Vous album is playing on a cassette in the Alfa's stereo. When it's our turn to go through the Silverstone gates, Bev cheerily chats to the steward as he hands him the tickets and he buys a programme that he passes back to me, which I accept, gratefully. Neil's gone back to sleep, he's not a very big F1 fan, he only really likes fishing. It's about nine o'clock when we park up just behind the bank that runs behind Stowe and Club corners.

We immediately start unloading the scaffolding (that we have borrowed from a builder in the village, who had done some work on our house), and lug the metal poles and wooden planks up to the top of the bank. There are quite a few fans already sat around in garden chairs and in groups on chequered picnic blankets; there is not a cloud in the sky and the July sun is already hot enough to give me a bit of a sweat on, as I plonk a wooden plank onto the grass.

By eleven o'clock dad and Bev have built our magnificent viewing platform, where the six of us will be able to watch the Grand Prix in comfort; whilst the hordes of other fans are packed in like sardines, a few feet below us. A few support races have taken place, and the F1 thoroughbreds have had their final warm-up before the race, that is due to start at two o'clock. My banner hangs off the front of our stand.

By twelve noon the grandstands and viewing banks around us are full. Sat in our lofty positon, on blankets and comfortable cushions, we have a fine view of The Hanger straight (where the Grand Prix cars will approach two-hundred miles an hour). We will be able to see them take Stowe corner at incredible speed, fly passed us, before they brake for Club corner (the ninety degree right-hander) and watch them burst up the hill towards the left-handed kink at Abbey curve, where we watched James Hunt win the race from, two years earlier. We can see about a quarter of the whole track, which is glorious, and I am getting super excited now.

As the start approaches, the Formula One cars file passed at irregular intervals to line up on the grid, where they will turn off their engines and sit for thirty minutes or so until the start. Alan Jones goes passed us in the Williams, he is in pole position and clear favourite for this race. The lemon yellow Renaults go by; the flat sound of their turbo engines contrast with the higher pitched Ford Cosworth V8 power units in most of the other cars. But you have to cover your ears when Villeneuve, in the beautiful red Ferrari, screams passed; the V12 behind him wailing in protest, as he floors the throttle coming out of Stowe corner. He then, immediately, tests his brakes down into Club corner and gets the car a bit snaky. His car control is immense, even though this is just the relatively slow, grid formation lap. I am stood up, open mouthed, my tongue is slightly hanging out; a bit like a cartoon character.

The black Lotus go by, followed by the dark red and blue Brabham Alfas; Bev, stood next to me, gives me a smile. Scheckter, in the other scarlet Ferrari, drives gently passed, blipping the throttle. Next through is a Shadow, with what sounds like a rough engine, then the Marlboro McLarens and blue Ligiers go by to add to the already colourful spectacle. Patrese's Arrows is the last to pass us, making up the grid. Twenty minutes to blast off.

The Red Arrows do their stuff in the blue skies above. A

Harrier Jump Jet takes off vertically, just in front of us, takes a bow, whilst hovering, and then roars off over Northamptonshire countryside. Three minutes to the start: the grid (although we can't see it from our position) will soon be cleared, leaving just the twenty-five or so courageous little men, lying almost flat, in their fat-wheeled rockets, revving their engines, eyes wide.

Alan Jones, the brave Australian, will be hoping that today he can be victorious, and win the first Grand Prix ever for his Williams team. He leads the field around on their final formation lap. My beloved Ferrari have qualified way down the grid in eleventh and thirteenth positions; this British track clearly not suiting their Italian chassis for some reason.

Everyone is standing now. Even mum and Neil – not the biggest race fans – can't help but be excited. Some fans are trying to climb up our scaffolding, but dad and Bev politely tell them to, "Piss off." They clamber down, apologetically.

The track commentator (talking in a voice that sounds like we should be watching the whole thing in black and white) is drowned out, as thousands of horsepower is unleashed from the grid. We can hear it, but we can't see them, not yet. It takes about thirty-five seconds before I see the first cars appear through the heat haze under the Hanger straight bridge. The racing speed that they take the right-hand corner at Stowe, is mind boggling.

Jones leads, followed by the French Renault. Regazzoni, in the other Williams car, is right up there; the rest of the pack screams passed, amongst them, somewhere, I see the flashes of the blood red Ferraris. Once the last car disappears through Abbey curve, and out of sight, there is a relative quiet, just a faint rumble, as the cars pass the start/finish straight to complete their first lap. In the blink of an eye though, the cars appear again; Jones passes us, already extending his lead over Frenchman Jean-Pierre Jabouille in the Renault; the rest of the field rushes passed, already beginning to spread out. The engine smells fill my nostrils as the engine noise rattles my chest.

I feel a bit sorry for the stragglers at the back of the field, falling quickly behind, almost like they are in a different race from the front runners. They are quickly lapped by the leaders.

By halfway, Jones, who has been looking like he could win this race driving a milk float, suddenly conks out, and drives slowly passed us with smoke coming from the back of his white and green car. Second place man, Jabouille, in the Renault is also out. Clay Regazzoni, the Swiss/Italian (who looks like he could do no other job than be a racing driver), takes up the lead and easily wins the 1979 British Grand Prix, ahead of the remaining Renault, driven by Rene Arnoux. By the end of the race it is all a bit spread out. Villeneuve's Ferrari drops out on lap sixty-three and team mate, Jody Scheckter, comes home fifth, but miles behind the winner. Williams win their first ever race and although the Ferraris have been a disappointment, it's been a great day; another great day, and I've loved it.

It's five forty-five in the afternoon and I am nodding off in the comfortable, bucket seats of Annie and Bev's Alfa Romeo. It's warm and I am super sleepy after a long, but brilliant day. My head keeps falling forward and waking me up, but I realise I've still got a smile on my face. I've been dreaming, dreaming that I am Gilles Villeneuve's new team mate: dressed in red overalls, stood with one foot on the sidepod of my Ferrari, racing gloves tucked in my helmet. I am chatting, casually, to my race engineer in the pits at Monaco; beautiful women are hanging around...

Chapter 32

Diary: 9.15am Thursday 17th April 2003

I *think this is what it is like to be imprisoned for a crime you haven't committed. I felt like this as I washed up my single plate, knife and fork in the kitchen sink at Clic house. I shouldn't be here, at least I should be at home with my boy, my little puppy dog, Alex.*

So, it's about a week since I last wrote. This coincides with Louise, me and Emma all being at Clic house since last Friday. 6 days and nights off the ward. It was great initially, but extremely hard work after a couple of days. Not being surrounded by 24 hour care is stressful. We had to go into the ward everyday anyway, for her to be checked and have her meds, but it was tough. Perhaps I'm becoming institutionalised.

Yesterday when we were on the ward, I saw a group of people as I was bringing some tea back for Louise and me. They were all laughing with the doctor and nurses. They were clearly the family of a 'survivor' and were indeed 'survivors' themselves. They were back for a check-up, I guess, but it felt like a gloat. I despised them. I'm sorry but I did. As they were leaving (the dad slapping a male nurse on the back and sharing a joke) I heard the mother say, "Thank God we're not still in here." They are right, of course, but it made me feel like shit. I didn't tell Louise.

Kind Dr. Khan wasn't happy with Emma's weight, so they planned to pump her full of 'space food' once her Hickman line goes in on Thursday. Which is today, isn't it?

Diary: 11pm Thursday 17th April 2003

I cried when they took her to theatre this afternoon to put her 'wiggly' long line in. I think I was alright until one of the theatre staff put her hand on my shoulder and said, "It will be OK" – I think that's what she said, she might have said nothing.

When we were leaving the anaesthetic room, the other theatre nurse said "Don't worry, I'll look after her." They did too. She has a smart 'wiggly' sticking out of her chest on the left-hand side. They will be able to put drugs and 'space food' down that line, straight into her bloodstream, and take blood out without constantly looking for tiny veins in her hands, arms and legs. That's the theory anyway.

Back to last Tuesday, Neil and his partner Anne came up from London. They were going to stay with her parents in Somerset about an hour away. And so with Anne driving, Neil and I had a few pints of SPA pale bitter in the Hare on the Hill. Nice.

Yesterday, Alex came with Louise's mum and dad and he was pretty moody, unlike him, but we played monsters in the Clic house garden – Billy (Emma's fellow cancer inmate) was on day release and he played with Alex, until he got too tired. I gave Alex a present, a model of 'Diesel 10' from Thomas The Tank Engine. He loved it.

Christ, it has been boiling hot the last few days. Mum and dad came on Monday. Dad and I went for a couple of pints in the Hare on the Hill, my new 'local'. Dad and I talked about Queen Elizabeth I. He knows so much about history and I'm starting to show some interest; although you could say twenty years too late, if you looked at my 'O' level history result.

This past week is all jumbled up.

I talked about the cancer with my brother, Neil, when he came up. A proper, sensible, sober talk (even though we were in the pub). I hadn't done that before. I could tell he was horrified.

Neil came with us to the ward when he was here last week. He was minding Emma when I went to get some coffees. When I got back the nurses were around the bed, with Neil standing a few feet away looking worried. Emma had relieved herself of her drip, by ripping the cannula

164

out of her hand. It's not a pleasant thing and I could see Neil was a bit shocked. I was calm, more worried about Neil. Again, I felt like a veteran of these unpleasant things that my daughter is having to suffer.

Neil and I went for some walks up and down the corridors of level 6. We talked about the Iraq war, his job, and the film 'Sexy Beast' that was on Channel 4 a couple of nights ago. We were both particularly impressed with Ben Kingsley and his character's use of the word 'cunt' throughout his cameo.

It is light relief when I see Neil, in particular.

I did the same walk with dad the other day as well (although we didn't talk about 'Sexy Beast!'). Dad got strangely confused when we reached the end of the corridor. We turned around to head back and he genuinely tried to open some linen cupboard doors, thinking that they were the doors back to the ward. I'm a bit concerned about him, although the episode was mildly amusing.

Emma is always hungry now. It's the steroids they say. Because of her insatiable appetite for fists full of cheesy crisps and snacks, I have nicknamed her after a new Tim Burton character: 'Emma Quaver Hands.'

Back to today, Thursday. We were back on ward 34's main ward (we were kicked out of our side room today) and it was boring and tiring, irritating and stressful. I fucking hated it. Louise was planning to go out tonight with her friend, Jackie, but I couldn't stay on the ward with Emma tonight. I just couldn't do it. I don't apologise for it either. Louise had to cancel and I'm sure she is as fucked off as I am, but I just could not do it tonight.

The tellies on the ward are so loud. I know I've forgiven the parents before for this inconsiderate behaviour but I can't deal with it tonight. It has just got to me; I will flip. So I'm back at Clic house writing this.

No smiles off Emma for weeks.

Good night darling.

Diary: 10.45pm Easter Monday 21st April 2003

Last Friday was really bad. Couldn't sleep on the ward with Emma again. The boy called Allister kept shouting that he wanted to go home. He is about 8 or 9 years old. It put me back in the trenches again. Only this time, Allister is a fallen soldier, screaming in no man's land, half dead, begging for mercy. You can hear him, but you can't help him.

You can't help him because you have to try and preserve yourself. You have to stay strong, so that you can help your own little one when the time comes. Allister doesn't get my help. It makes me feel like a coward.

I changed over shifts with Louise on Saturday morning, walked back up the hill to Clic house in a tearful daze, half hoping to be knocked over by a bus. Cried in the kitchen, needed comforting from Billy's mum (who was witnessing my distress), but it didn't come. Cried again in the parents room. Christ, how many tears can a grown man shed!

Came back to the ward in the afternoon after a half-sleep, to the news that we had been moved back to a side room - small miracle - I couldn't have done another night on the ward.

Had a better Saturday evening, Neil came down especially from London and took me out for a couple of drinks. We watched 'A Texas Chainsaw Massacre' back in the room at Clic house, it seemed appropriate.

Sunday, yesterday, was a better day. I'm clearly really down when I'm so tired. Emma's tum has been bloated again since Friday night (another stressful x-ray revealed just gas — uncomfortable but not life threatening). But when we got back from x-ray she sat on the bed for the first time in weeks and played with a wooden puzzle and I got a smile out of her.

She got a temperature later on though, and her bloody long line didn't work when they needed to take blood to check if she has another infection. Andy, the Aussie doctor had to needle stick her in the arm, but he did it quickly to his credit. We wait and see if she'll need another bucket of sickening antibiotics, to fight yet another infection.

My dad's not too well, but he and mum came up again to the Forest to look after Alex all week. Louise's parents had him over the weekend. No one can visit Emma at the moment (apart from Louise and I), she is too at risk of infection.

Played a bit more with her today, Monday, on the bed. She is looking pretty tubby in the face now. It's the steroids they say! She is being given this high calorie, high protein, high everything 'space food' directly into her veins via the long line. Today they had to stop one of these bags of feed because there was something wrong with her liver test. Just a precaution they said.

***

"I'll darn your socks, I'll stitch you up when you're wounded and I'll do what you tell me. But I won't watch you die. I'll miss that scene if you don't mind." That's what Katherine Ross's character just said to Butch and Sundance as I watched this film classic back at Clic house tonight. I'm not sure I will get that luxury.

I hope your temperature has gone down and I'll see you in the morning my darling.

Chapter 33

Down the river

Me and Tom have done some pretty silly things, but it doesn't get much sillier than some of the stuff we have done during this, our last, summer holiday as primary school kiddies. It's August 1979 and as usual the holidays have been hot and fun, such fun.

Let's start with coin squashing shall we? Remember that railway line that runs from Oxford to Kenbury: the one that passes under 'Dean Taylor's bridge,' the one that saw Tom's brother lose his tooth, well, that railway line is really easy to get onto.

Now, me and Tom have seen those public information films on the telly about titting around in the countryside and dying, but they seem to have made very little impact on these particular eleven year old boys. It seems that after watching these three minute films (about the dangers of flying a kite by a pylon, or mucking about on farms and falling into shit pits, or, in particular, walking about on railway lines), we instantly forget they are warning us about something bad.

So, it is without a second thought, that we scramble down the steep embankment, get some two pence pieces out of our jeans' pockets, place them directly on the railway line and put our ears to the tracks to hear if a train is coming. If the track starts to ring, you scramble into the bushes and hold your breath as the eleven forty-five from Oxford comes screaming by within about ten feet of you. Then, knowing that another train isn't due for an hour, we scavenge amongst the railway line stones to try and find our squashed coins. Moronic, yes, I know; but massive fun. If our mums ever found out, we would be better off being hit by a locomotive.

Or, how about this for silliness, as the final days of the holidays tick on by? A new, small, wooden footbridge had sprung up one day down the river. The little bridge didn't span the river Evenlode itself, but a small stream that feeds it. The bridge, as far as me and Tom could tell, served absolutely no purpose whatsoever. It didn't come from anywhere important and it didn't appear to go anywhere important: useless. So useless in fact, that we decide to take a couple of screwdrivers and some spanners from our dads' (not so extensive) toolkits, and disassemble the new bridge.

Not only do we disassemble the bridge, once we have done so, we sail the thing down the stream, until it gets stuck in a tree overhanging the brook. Madness, yes, I know, but hugely entertaining. When a woman walked passed us with her dog and asked us what we were doing, Tom looked up at her and confidently said, "We are the sons of carpenters," and casually went about unscrewing the bolt that secured the bridge to the bank. The woman looked at me, slightly startled, but I just nodded. She walked off, presumably speechless.

More craziness? How about this? Back to the railway line. Up each side of the embankment is some wire mesh, about thirty feet high, I guess it's for holding the bricks together or something. It's a straightforward race to see who can climb up the quickest. I don't normally win this, Tom is like a monkey at climbing and pretty fearless. It's a bit like the lava game that we used to play up Tom's stairs, just much more dangerous. Once we've both got to the top, we lie in the grass on our backs, laughing, breathless in the late summer sun.

Not everything we do is reckless though. We're not that naughty. When other kids from school are out playing, we all make our way to forty-forty mountain. To get to forty-forty mountain you have to cross that railway bridge, walk over the meadow down by the river, cross the stream (well, jump the stream, there is no bridge there now) and walk through the woods, where you suddenly come across this gorgeous, secluded opening in the trees. Here be forty-forty mountain.

Alright, it's not a mountain, it's a little, steep hill, covered in soft long grass. Forty-forty is a game that is played here, but we mostly play Best Man Dead and Army. My best, Best Man Dead, is pretending to be a German soldier in the film Hannibal Brooks, when 'Lucy' (Oliver Reed's elephant), pulls down the Nazi's log cabin check point in the Alps, and the soldiers come tumbling down the mountain.

"What weapon do you want to die by?" Tom would shout up from the bottom of the hill, when it is my turn to be killed in a game of Best Man Dead."

"Elephant!" I shout back.

We build camps as well, of course. This summer we have only built the one, but it is top drawer. Well hidden, about two-hundred yards further on from forty-forty mountain, in a hard to get to bit of undergrowth, we have built a den with two rooms: a kitchen and a living room. It has a roof that is made from branches and it is camouflaged in ferns.

To stop anyone entering our den, we have placed a number of trip wires around the entrance to the camp, with bells attached, so that we can hear if anyone is coming. If the invaders decide not to heed the bells as a warning, we have put some sharpened sticks in the ground, so if they trip over they are likely to get impaled on them. If they are lucky, we might show them mercy and release them; depends who it is though. No one's found this camp yet, luckily for them!

The last few days of the summer holidays of 1979 are upon us. Secondary school is a reality now. Mum's got my school uniform and a pair of vile, black shoes and a rather poofy black brief case. I guess I am getting a little nervous, but Tom will be there as well, so we can look after each other.

Me and Tom are off to Craveley secondary school, about five miles away (it's the school where my brother goes) and hopefully me and Tom will be in the same class. We don't know anyone else that goes to this school, except my brother Neil, who unkindly told me that the school is massive, and that I will get lost, for sure. He said that one-thousand-five-hundred children go to the school. I worked out that's one-thousand-four-hundred-and-forty more children than go to my primary school; thanks for that, brother.

Most of the other boys from primary school are going to a school in Kenbury, about five miles in the opposite direction. It is a bit of a shame, but we'll cope, me and Tom.

Chapter 34

Diary: Friday 25th April 2003

*H*er temperature had gone down by Tuesday morning but she has got another bug since then. It is endless. The 'wiggly' line that, undoubtedly, helps with giving her drugs, food, and taking blood, also hinders her because she gets infections off it. It's not surprising either; it's made of plastic and metal and it sticks out of a little girl's skin, who has zero immunity to fight infections.

They have given her some very specific antibiotics but her temps have been sky high, particularly in the early evening.

Emma's nose feeding tube has been out for a few days because they were feeding her down her long line. However, Nurse Kate had insisted that it goes back in, because at the moment they aren't using the long line to feed her because of all the infections. Kate got her way with the doctor and put the tube down Emma's nose efficiently and without too much fuss. Kate's a star.

Beth, the dietitian, turned up and explained the feeding process down the nose tube. All seemed very sensible. I have to say, Emma is looking a bit brighter. Playing peek-a-boo with me under the sheets and I got lots of smiles! It is so good to see.

She loves these wooden puzzles, 'Connect 4' (yes, I always win because she doesn't understand the rules) and 'Hungry Pussy Cats' (she is better at that one).

Heather the physio' has got her an upright pushchair and we've been doing some corridor touring. Emma's stopped this constant moaning that she had been doing for ages and although she still seems a bit fractious (and now doesn't eat anything herself, not even Quavers), I think she is looking OK. Apart from having a large, bloated head!

I've felt much better over the past couple of days. And it is a big help writing this diary. The Big Cheese, Professor Elmwood, didn't even come around today. Hope that's a good sign and they're not too worried about her at the moment.

Met another A.L.L today, just in, called Sam. He is two years old. Talked a bit to his worried mum and dad yesterday. It seemed strange me answering some of their questions about A.L.L. Good luck Sam.

Heard some bad stuff about some of the other kids on the ward yesterday. Joseph has got a one-in-two chance and Matthew has a lump on his liver.

Evie, by all accounts, is the miracle child. She was supposed to go home (proper home) today, but she was still on the ward when I left for Clic tonight. It is never over, 'til it's over!

Emma did a bit of podgy-faced head dancing to 'Incy Wincey spider' yesterday. Mum and dad had brought in a tape recorder from home. Dad's much better, but mum's got a cold now, but seems OK. They are doing a bloody marvellous job looking after Alex. Dad said he is such a lovely kid. He is too.

I've got this feeling today that it might just be a long waiting game this – an anxious, fretful waiting game. But I'm trying not to think too far ahead. Just weeks and days, not bone marrow transplants, intensive care and, well, death. I'm just giving myself a breather from all that for a while.

My great mates, brothers Jack and Richie are coming tomorrow. I shall get drunk and forget for a few hours.

Emma's blood was dark red tonight. That's OK isn't it?

Good night my darling.

Diary: 10.20pm Thursday 1ˢᵗ or 2ⁿᵈ May 2003

Dark blood is OK apparently. Seems like a long time ago, that particular worry.

We lost little Matthew yesterday. He was Emma's age. Don't know how to feel really. Very sad for the parents, but didn't know them at all. I thought of it like some sort of macabre game for an instant today. Matthew's out, Emma's still in.

I finally picked up enough courage to ask my percentage question of the doctors. The answer: it looks like she still has just a 75% chance of survival over the full 5 years (that's 5 years after the treatment has finished). I still don't quite get it though, what's the point of all those tests that come back bringing good news, if it doesn't push up her chances of survival!

I'll try and forget about it for now.

Emma's been pretty good all week, Louise bought her some new PJ's. Dr. Jim put a new nose tube in her today – it's a much longer tube and easier for putting things down it. I picked her up from theatre today on my own (must have been feeling all brave or something), when she had her lumber puncture. They said her breathing was a bit fast though, which was something I didn't need to hear.

I lost her bloody teddy bear yesterday. How could that be allowed to happen? The only thing she gets a bit of comfort from. I must have wrapped it up in a dirty sheet and it got thrown away. Idiot.

More physio' today with Heather in the side room. Tomorrow, hopefully, we can go to the physio' department because Emma's not got a bug. It would be a nice change of scene.

We sat in our room with the door open and watched the ward go by, me and Emma, today. It was nice to see Dr. Jim back again, he has been away for a bit. At the end of the day Dr. Jo got a smile off my little darling and she came in to say it had made her day after a bad shift. It made me happy and I joked with Dr. Jo that as no one else had seen the smile, it couldn't be verified - but Dr. Simmons, the other SHO, backed her up.

The play specialist is called Tina, and she got loads of new toys for Emma today. Tina is the only member of staff who calls me by my name.

Louise said she doesn't ever want us to move into side room No.4, where we lost poor Matthew. I think I agree.

Good night my darling.

Diary: 10.30pm Friday 2nd May 2003

I forgot to mention my friends, the brothers, Jack and Richie. They came, they saw, we got drunk. It was good to see them. Emma was just great tonight, almost normal... apart from having a massive balloon face, a hosepipe sticking out of her nose, she can't walk and having fucking cancer!

Jonathan Ross on the telly tonight with Madonna.

Today I got all worried about the next bone marrow test coming up. It's a big one, really important.

Emma pulled her nose tube out again last night. Kirsty and the educational nurse with the good haircut, tried to put it back in, but they couldn't do it. I got a bit cross. Emma was in a lot of discomfort. Sister Kate came a bit later and did it in super quick time.

I like Sister Kate. There I've said it, I won't mention it again.

Diary: Wednesday 7th May 2003

I've been to the Hare on the Hill again and had three pints of Becks. It's sort of becoming my day off thing to do, and it's kinda getting me through really. I can't seem to sit and read or listen to music or occupy myself at the moment, so I may as well numb the pain a bit. I watched a bit of the champion's league semi-final, first leg (Milan 0 – Inter 0): a good, old, Italian classic.

Her hair has gone! It came out in about 2 days. That will be the Vincristine drug. She looks OK though, my little peachy head. I cut off a lock of her hair before it all fell out and wrapped it in a bit of paper with a picture of 'Spot the Dog' on it, and put it in my wallet. Also when she is asleep, I put my mouth close to hers and when she breathes out, I breathe in. I do this so that I will always have her breath inside me, just in case she, well, you know, just in case.

Emma's been, well, fantastic. Lots of smiles from her as we, again, watched the doctors and nurses go by from our side room. Nurse Kate said she would get Emma put on the payroll, because she is making everyone happy. Dr. Golden saw us yesterday, he is a bloody nice bloke, reckoned he could get us back to Clic house for a few days maybe next week (although we didn't cope that well being away from the hospital last time we were released).

Emma's temperature is down. Can't remember if I said she had another infection, she has them all the time, poor thing. They can be really dangerous. They treat them with various antibiotics, she gets better for about a day, and then gets another spiked temperature, and we go through it all again.

Louise got really cross with Nurse 'Ratched' last Saturday. She is just a crap nurse compared to all the others. She's a miserable bitch, unhelpful and thoughtless. I punched the wall in the side room, she pissed me off so much. Emma was being sick again from the chemo' and this nurse was super unhelpful.

Anyway, we've had a good few days really. Heather the physio' got her walking on a mini-walker with wheels today on floor 7. Bloody great to see! She's all pink in the face now and well, kinda healthy looking I suppose. She's got a chance right?

It's her second bone marrow test tomorrow. Nervous. It's the really important one.

Alex came today with mum and dad. It is the longest we've not seen him. We took him to the park and played in the sandpit. Louise stayed with Emma. It was so nice to see him. We played monsters. I can't wait to get home, whenever that will be.

Good night my darlings.

Thursday 8th May 2003

Had the bone marrow test in theatre today. Results expected tomorrow.

Good night my darling.

Friday 9th May 2003

No results from the test. It should have come back today.

Saturday 10th May 2003

None of the regular doctors on shift today, no one could tell me about the test results. Shit.

Sunday 11th May 2003

Still no results from the test. When I asked Dr. Jim, he looked away slightly when he said they were still looking at it. I couldn't catch his eye for the rest of the day. Concerned.

Fran Gabaldoni

Monday 12 May 2003

Dr. Jim has said that Professor Elmwood needs to come and talk to us first thing in the morning about Emma's bone marrow test. I'm pretty much paralysed now with worry.

Chapter 35

Jessica Wakeman

Jessica Wakeman has something called a brain tumour. I don't quite know what that is, but apparently it is really serious. My mum sat me down yesterday evening (I thought I'd done something wrong) and she told me that Jessica was very poorly. I didn't quite know what to do. I had felt sad a few years ago when my grandma, my dad's mother, had died, but I didn't know her very well and I was very young. This was different. This felt like a big shock, something happening that shouldn't happen.

"Is she going to die?" I'd asked my mum.

Mum looked away slightly, "Er, she's very poorly," she repeated.

Were Mr and Mrs Wakeman going to lose their pretty little daughter, their only child, my May Queen? I had thought as I went into the kitchen. Gosh, that really is terrible. That shouldn't happen to anyone. I felt a bit sick in my tummy.

***

Today I went around to Tom's but he wasn't in. I wanted to know if he had heard any more about Jessica. Mr Tate answered the door and said that Tom had gone with his mum to Kenbury. He shut the door gently, and as I walked back down The Passage in the drizzle, on my own, I wondered what Tom might be doing in Kenbury with his mum. When I got home I wandered around the house: Neil was out fishing, dad was at work, mum was busy. I was bored.

I called back around to Tom's at about five thirty that afternoon. The Tates were just finishing their tea, but Mrs Tate invited me in anyway, though she looked a little serious. Tom gave me a weak smile as I entered the dining room, but he didn't really look at me.

"Alright Tom?" I said, sitting on the chair that Mrs Tate had pulled up for me.

"Yeah, I'm OK," he replied quietly. There was a silence. I fiddled with a spoon.

"Did you hear about Jessica Wakeman?" I asked, eventually.

"Yes, it is terribly sad," said Mr Tate, placing his knife and fork together on his plate. There was another silence. There was never a silence around this table. I felt my tummy churning again.

"We've got something we need to tell you," said Mrs Tate. "I've mentioned it to your mum, but I thought we should tell you now." My eyes widened, I felt a bit faint. Tom shuffled in his chair.

After a slight pause, Mrs Tate continued. "Tom and I went to Kenbury today," she paused again. "You see, well, we've decided that Tom is going to go to Kenbury secondary school next year, and, and, I know that will come as a bit of a shock to you, because you are obviously going to Craveley school, aren't you, and Tom was going to go there as well, but, you see, we've decided that Kenbury is, well...." Mrs Tate couldn't finish her sentence, she could see I was welling up a little, staring into the centre of the dining table.

"That's OK," I said finally, "We'll see each other after school and weekends and that, won't we Tom?"

Tom was still looking down into his half-eaten dinner.

"I guess so," he said quietly.

"Anyway, I need to get back for my tea," I lied, and I pushed my chair back carefully, said my goodbyes and stumbled down the steps of the Tate's house, across the road, passed our primary school and headed down The Passage in a teary daze.

"You'll meet new friends at your new school, it will be alright," my mum said when I got home, giving me a hug. I knew that it wouldn't; nothing would be quite the same again.

Chapter 36

I'm back in a hospital again. I'm in an outpatient's audiology department in the hearing test room. It's mid afternoon, and it is hot and I'm sleepy and it reminds me of that terrible day, twelve years earlier, when I was told that my poor, baby daughter, Emma, had leukaemia.

The audiology technician gently taps his computer mouse to register beeps that go into the patient's headphones. You have to press a button every time you pick up a beep, to make sure that you can hear at different frequencies.

Wearing the headphones is a pretty, slim, fourteen year old girl with beautiful, strawberry blond hair. She is sitting on a chair in the corner of the room, intently pressing a button every time she hears a beep.

"OK there, that's the end of the test," the technician says, in a soft, southern Irish accent. "Let's take those fellows off," and he points to the headphones. Emma removes the cans from her head, straightens her long hair with her left hand, looks up and smiles at me. I can tell that she is pleased because she thinks she did well in the test; she enjoys doing well at stuff.

So, she made it. She really made it. A survivor. One of the lucky ones, if you can call getting and then surviving leukaemia as a baby, 'lucky'.

On that nerve-racking day, back in May 2003, we had waited all morning for Professor Elmwood to come and tell us about Emma's second bone marrow test. I had tried to gear myself up for the bad news as best as I could. But the fight had gone out of me by that stage, I was spent, and I was certain that the news would be the start of the end in our battle with Emma's cancer. It was a desolate feeling.

When Professor Elmwood finally came to see us, he sat Louise and I down and told us that Emma's bone marrow test result was indeed cause for concern. It was serious, but as we came to learn over the next ten years, every twist and turn with this spiteful illness was serious.

Apparently, the test had shown that the leukaemia cells had not been fully eradicated as they had first thought. It was not, however, Professor Elmwood reassured us, by any means a reason to alter her treatment. By contrast, he had said, they would continue, relentlessly, with the chemotherapy.

Emma's infections continued to be terrible and at times, life threatening. She had to have her Hickman line removed at least three times because the infections it gave her were so bad, they could have killed her.

Today she is left with scars on her chest, where the 'wiggly' Hickman lines made such a mess of her skin, and it simply could not heal. We were told, a couple of years later, that she could have some plastic surgery if she wanted to make the scars look better. To date, Emma has said she's not bothered. "They're my battle scars, Dad," she says, although in reality, she says she can't remember much about the battle. Thankfully, Nurse Kate was right about that, all those years ago.

Her ears also got dreadfully infected, as her immune system continued to be unable to fight the bacteria over the next three years. Her left ear drum is permanently perforated and that's the reason why we are sat in the hearing test room today, in the audiology department at Gloucester Royal Hospital. Her hearing is slightly down on power, but no hearing aids will be necessary, they tell us.

Emma stayed in Bristol Children's Hospital for a further three months; sometimes we had a side room, sometimes we were on the ward. We went home once in that time, but she got a temperature almost immediately and we had to drive her straight back into Bristol. "Welcome back," Dr. Jim had said as I carried her back onto the ward. I couldn't help but smile, we had only been gone for twelve hours.

In August 2003, we got handed back into the care of Gloucester Hospital, where she had been originally diagnosed, six months before. It was a very emotional time, saying goodbye to the staff on ward thirty-four in Bristol, not knowing if we would see them again. If we did see them again, I guess it would mean that Emma had relapsed. But that didn't happen and we got just as good care in Gloucester as we had in Bristol. A new group of superstars carried on caring for our little girl. A new Professor Elmwood, a new Dr. Jim, a new Nurse Kate, all stepped up and got us through.

The next six months, up to Christmas 2003, saw Emma going back and forth to Gloucester Hospital. Sometimes this was routine, for her medicine and blood tests; other times it was because she had another infection, which needed to be treated immediately with antibiotics. As soon as she had a temperature, Louise and I knew that it would mean at least another week's stay in hospital. It was devastatingly hard. You could not plan anything. We did arrange a little trip away, to Devon for a couple of nights, in the spring, perhaps a year after she was diagnosed; but she got ill the day before and we couldn't go.

Her liquid feed was also a nightmare. Many times (particularly in the early days when we got her back home), the tube that her feed was pumped into, would pull out of her nose tube, flood the bed, and she would wake up, soaked in the sticky, sickly, high calorie, yellow liquid. By the time Louise and I had uncoupled her from her equipment, changed her pyjama's, turned the mattress over for the hundredth time, got her (and usually Alex) settled back to sleep, it was pretty much time for us to get up. It was exhausting.

Whilst Emma tended to be in good spirits when she didn't have an infection, as soon as she did, she would be in serious discomfort, irritable and grisly. The enormous amounts of antibiotics she had to have, would upset her tummy and the steroids and chemotherapy pretty much did for her appetite.

Slowly, the intensive medical regime was reduced, and with it, the temperatures and infections got slightly less frequent; although they were never far away. She contracted shingles, which was always on the cards, and was desperately poorly for a few days.

A nurse came to the house everyday to start with: she would take Emma's blood, send it off for testing, administer her medicine, adjust the dosage dependant on her blood results. This went on for the first few months.

After about a year and a half, in the summer of 2004, Emma's treatment was reduced again. Her blood counts were generally good (as long as she didn't have an infection), and the nurse started to come every other day, rather than daily. The trips to hospital became less frequent: once a week, then once a fortnight, then once a month.

Louise and I were taught how to administer Emma's drugs down her Hickman line. We used a needle and a syringe, to effectively, put the drugs directly into her bloodstream, and it was very scary at first. But we soon became proficient, and it saved us endless trips to the hospital. We were already both experts at giving her chemotherapy and steroids down her nose tube.

Emma was still very puffy in the face, and still had the fat, yellow feeding tube down her nose. The visual signs that she was still very poorly, made it very hard to forget how bad it all was.

She still had no hair, but slowly, very slowly, as the Vincristine drug was given less and less frequently, her hair began to grow back. All over her perfectly shaped head, her hair started to appear, evenly, over her scalp. Tiny indications that she was getting healthier. Tiny rays of light, which lifted my heart.

But my anxieties about her survival were never far from my mind. I thought I might need to go and see someone about it, but I never did. My apprehensions didn't go overnight; they just slowly diminished as the days, weeks, months and now years have gone by, and, as we were told, the likelihood of relapse became less and less likely. I had finally put my faith in the statistics. Five years after we gave Emma her final dose of chemotherapy, we were told that she was now as likely to get leukaemia as any other child. It was strangely reassuring.

Her visits to the hospital for blood tests became twice yearly for a bit, then once a year, until her consultant casually said, when she was eleven years old, "We won't need to see Emma again." There was no celebration, just relief.

Emma had survived, but unfortunately, my marriage hadn't. It is hard to explain, because looking in on it, you would think a trauma like your daughter having cancer, would pull a couple together. But it doesn't work like that. They are separate events; at least that is how I reflect on it.

We divorced in 2010, it was painful, particularly for Louise. Emma dealt with it all better than Alex, but it wasn't easy for anyone. The children lived with me for half the time and now they are fourteen and sixteen, we let them choose where they want to be. I see them most days, as Louise and I only live five miles apart, still in the Forest. They have a stepbrother and sister now, whose mum I fell in love with. True love, is true love, right?

My mum and dad continued to live at Chatterpie Cottage in Lambe. We visited them every few months or so. It was the second hardest phone call I'd ever made (the hardest was telling them that Emma had leukaemia), when I called mum and dad to tell them I had left Louise. My dad was so surprised he immediately said, "Sorry, where have you left Louise?" The reality soon sunk in though, and although they found it difficult to comprehend at first (their marriage was as solid as ever), they supported me in the difficult months that followed, like they had always supported me. Later, they both fell in love with my new wife, as most people did.

Mum died of stomach cancer in 2009 and dad died of lung cancer in 2014. Neil and I were both with them to see them off. Heartbreaking.

Jessica Wakeman survived her brain tumour, but what turned out to be a benign lump, grew next to her optic nerve and she was, cruelly, left blind for life. The beautiful, young May Queen, who danced and laughed with me on that fateful, but ultimately hilarious May Day back in 1979, was robbed of her sight at eleven years old. It was tragic in the extreme. The strain on her mum and dad was terrible. As a parent, I guess, I got off lightly by comparison.

In September 1979, Tom Tate, my best mate, went off to Kenbury comprehensive and I went off to Craveley secondary school. It was hard not seeing him everyday, sharing our experiences in our brave new worlds. But we both made new friends at our new schools, and life wasn't as painful as I thought it was going to be. It wasn't quite the same though, when we saw each other at weekends and sometimes after school; but maybe that was just more about growing up, rather than growing apart.

Kenbury school actually closed when Tom was starting his 'O' level year, and so he ended up coming to join me at Craveley anyway (albeit four years after he should have!). I welcomed him into my life there, as I knew he would, if my school had shut down.

Tom did pretty well in his exams, but he couldn't decide what to do. He flitted about on different courses: some 'A' levels, agricultural college, finally ending up at Southampton Polytechnic as a mature student. He couldn't settle into a job after that, or relationships very well. We kept in touch, and often caught up when I went back to see my mum and dad; he was still living at home with his parents. They continued to live in Lambe, but now in a rather soulless bungalow since they had moved out of their family home, Moss Barn, where Tom and I had grown up. Tom drifted from job to job; did a bit of teaching and ambulance driving, but he couldn't stick at anything for long periods.

In 2004, unexpectedly, he arranged to come and see me at our home in the Forest. He said he was keen to see how Emma was doing and it was lovely to see him. We went for a walk in the forest and he told me that he had found God. He was born again. I had started to take the piss, but quickly realised he was deadly serious.

"Are you happy?" I'd asked.

"I am," he said, thoughtfully.

"Good," I'd said and we went to the pub and got drunk.

He married a Czech girl a few years ago, but he told me that they would never have children. I didn't question him, but it was a shame, he would have been a fun dad.

In 2009, just before my mum died, Mr Tate, Tom's dad, also got taken by cancer. At his funeral, we all found out that he was not only the lovely, gentle bloke who taught RE and was my best friend's dad, but that he was also a decorated World War Two hero, who had fought, with distinction, for the Commandos in North Africa.

Me and Tom don't meet up as much as I would like to anymore; but when we do, even now, in our late forties, we still laugh about May Day, Halloween and bonfire nights, Han Solo and that tractor fire.

My life turned a bit of a corner after I knew I wasn't going to lose Emma. I dumped my relatively well paid, but ultimately boring job as a human resources manager, which I had taken up with a Council in Gloucester a few months after Emma got sick. I had no idea what I was I going to do, so I just paused, just for a bit. I took a breath.

I teach cricket now to kids in primary schools in the Forest. To say it's brilliant, would be an understatement. If I can encourage just one nine year old to play cricket up their drive, with their brother or sister, and smash the odd kitchen window, I'll die happy.

***

Emma's hearing test in audiology is all fine. We exit the hospital through the large automatic doors, and as we are walking back to the car park we pass a small bike shed, where hospital workers leave their push irons. I notice (because it is standing out so obviously amongst the expensive looking mountain bikes and colourful racers) an old fashioned bike with an enormous saddle. I smile, turning to Emma.

"You know my old mate, Tom Tate?" I say, putting my arm around her shoulders.

"Yes, of course," she replies.

"Well, did I ever tell you about that time we nicked his mum's bike?"

The End